The Chiseller

The Chiseller

TEX LARRIGAN

A Black Horse Western

ROBERT HALE · LONDON

Photoset in North Wales by
Derek Doyle & Associates, Mold, Flintshire
Printed and bound in Great Britain by
WBC Book Manufacturers Limited, Bridgend

The Chiseller

ONE

Saul Rhymer reached for his whiskey and took a
sip. He'd been drinking sparingly all night, but
now the time had come for the big break. His head
ached and his eyes were sore from the smoke of
the saloon's backroom. It seemed airless and what
there was, was foetid. Out of the dirty, curtainless
window the first streaks of dawn were breaking.
Soon, in a few hours, the steamboat *Star of the
West* would be leaving Fort Benton. He was determined to be on it.

The room was filled with sweaty, unwashed
men watching the play and the fortunes of the
four men sitting around the card table. Never had
there been such a pile of gold nuggets, dust and
greenbacks lying there and steadily growing. It
would be a story told for years to come.

It had been seven hours, and Saul's shoulders
were stiffened from being hunched over the cards
and his throat was dry for want of a good drink. It

wasn't whiskey he wanted, but a bucket of beer would have gone down well.

But it was nearly over.

Theodore Lang, the wealthiest man of the four, was becoming careless. He was too confident. Saul had manipulated the cards so that all four men won and lost in a regular succession. He himself had lost the most and it was deliberate for he was giving the impression of being a rookie at this game.

He was waiting for the big kill.

He leaned back in his chair and gave a nervous laugh.

'Well, gentlemen, as you see I'm down to my shirt.' He looked around at them all slowly, noting Lang's shaking hand. The fool had taken in too much whiskey. 'What say to one more hand?' He hesitated dramatically, then he announced softly, 'I'll lay my most treasured possession.'

'And what's that?' Theodore Lang leaned forward, a cigar clasped between his teeth. Saul shook his head regretfully.

'I hate to do this, but needs must when the devil drives.' He put a hand in his vest pocket and pulled out a folded piece of paper. 'There, gentlemen, is the deed to the richest gold-mine in the Yellowstone, goddammit!' He threw it with a flourish on top of the pile and the onlookers

8

The Chiseller

gasped as they saw the gilt-edged certificate.
Lang's eyes narrowed.

'Why aren't you up there working it?'

Saul shrugged his wide shoulders.

'Do I look like a miner? It was my father's last
wish that I carry on where he left off. Someday I
was going to do it, but now. . . .' He paused and
turned down his lips. 'I'm a betting man, mister,
and I can't resist that pot!'

'What do they call this mine?'

'The Charlotte Grace, in memory of my ma. See,
I've still got the first nugget my pa found in the
diggings at Bear Gulch.'

Lang's head came up when he heard Bear
Gulch. He made a quick decision.

'Right. How much?' Saul looked around at the
other two men and saw greed on their faces. 'I
reckon it's worth raising the ante.'

One of the men scowled and tossed in his cards.
'I pass.'

Lang chewed his cigar and considered his
cards. The fourth man looked at Lang and then
threw in his cards.

'Too meaty for me. I pass.'

Lang grinned and looked at Saul.

'Well, son, you've just lost yourself a gold-mine.
I raise you two thousand and call.' He laid his
cards face down and grinned in Saul's face. Saul
shrugged.

9

'Fair enough. I'm at the end of the line.' His lips twitched, but he managed to look rueful.

Lang spread his cards, two jacks, a queen and two nines, and made to grab the pot. A steely hand came out and grabbed his wrist.

'Just a minute. You haven't seen my hand.' The onlookers held their breath and leaned forward to see better. Saul slowly dropped his cards one by one on to the green baize, a running flush, ace high. The crowd gasped.

Shocked, Lang scowled. He thought he had the measure of the young fool before him. It must have been a fluke! Silently he watched Saul scoop up the mountain of gold, nuggets and paper money into his hat. Then he leaned forward and said softly, 'Gimme a break. I'll give you a thousand for that certificate of ownership. What d'you say?'

Saul pursed his lips and whistled and shook his head.

'It's worth more than that. It's my insurance for the future.'

'You said yourself you're no gold-miner. You're more suited to the tables. Besides, where'd you get the cash to get started?'

Saul gave a lift to his shoulders. 'I could get a partner.'

'Look, I'll give you two thousand and this bag of dust.' Lang reached into the pocket of his greatcoat and dropped a heavy bag on the table.

Saul loosened the drawstrings and tipped some of the contents into his hand. The gold dust gleamed dully in the early morning light. Outside came the first warning blast from the steamboat moored at the levee. Saul considered and then appeared to make up his mind reluctantly.

'You've persuaded me. It's a deal.' Lang grinned and they shook hands and Saul tossed him the certificate.

'Good luck, and now if you'll excuse me, I'm going to hunt up some breakfast.'

'We'll play again. What about tonight?'

'Yes, same time, same place. I'll look forward to it.' Then Saul was pushing his way through the crowd, his hat held tight to his chest.

Outside the saloon he took several deep breaths of cool fresh air. God! It had been tough! He made his way to the livery stable and stuffed everything into his saddle-bags. He would count the take later. He walked the horse outside and then, astride, put her to a gallop and headed for the levee.

As the wind whipped through his hair, exhilaration swept through him and he laughed out loud as he rode.

'You'll be lucky, Mr Lang! You can find yourself another sucker!'

Then he whistled a tuneless rendering of 'John

Brown's Body', pleased with his performance. God, it was like taking candy from a baby. In his mind he counted how many more forged certificates he had stashed in his saddle-bags. He wouldn't be able to play that scam on the steamboat. He would make the next killing in St Louis.

There was the last-minute bustle on the levee as the *Star of the West* was about to leave Fort Benton. Short sharp bursts of steam jetted from her and the captain stood on the bridge and yelled at the roustabouts hauling aboard the cargo. Bales of fur and buffalo hides were stowed in the cargo holds and also littered the lower deck to the disgust of passengers who fought for the best vantage points to bed down. There were no cabins on the lower deck. The paddle-steamer was designed for freight, not passengers, and those who travelled back to St Louis had to pay through the nose for the privilege, usually in gold. For those who travelled were men, some with womenfolk, who'd been out to the goldfields and struck lucky. Others were trappers or agents who bought up furs from the Indians or white hunters.

They were all tough and resourceful. They had to be to come up the great Missouri River in the first place. They'd fought the river in all its winding glory, faced the hazards of whitewater rapids and sandbanks, and hidden obstacles like trees uprooted and washed downriver during storms to become waterlogged and covered over with the mud and silt that came down from the far Rocky Mountains. Fort Benton was as far as the paddle-steamers could travel.

Those who could afford to go back were on the last great adventure to return to civilization. St Louis was the centre of the new world that was now booming in the West.

Men who had courage and strength and a ruth-less will could make it big . . . if they lived to go back East. Some did, some did not. Saul Rhymer was determined he'd go back to his roots a whiskey-drinking, cigar-smoking millionaire before he was forty, and show the Kansas neigh-bours that the local farm boy they'd drummed out of town could make good and buy them all out! He would show that snooty Mary Makkoy especially. He still smarted when he remembered her scorn-ful laughter.

'Walk out with you, Saul Rhymer? Why, you're the no-good son of the man who shot Sheriff Morgan! I wouldn't be seen dead beside you!'

But that had been a long time ago. Fifteen years to be exact and Mary's face was now just a blur. At least she'd been the spur to send him off on his quest to make his fortune.

He was called The Chiseller behind his back and was proud of the name. He never made a move without plotting out each detail and in the bank at St Louis, there was a deposit account in his name which proved he had been successful.

The priority now, he thought to himself as he took his horse aboard the steamer, was to protect his newfound wealth from any would-be have-a-go Joe who thought he had a better right to it. It was going to be a long hazardous journey, nearly 2,700 miles of treacherous river and even more treacherous passengers.

He'd survive, like hell he would!

He found a place for himself and his horse in a corner of the open deck area. There was cargo, huge stinking bales of badly cured furs, and between them, nooks and corners which the passengers claimed as their own.

They all grumbled at the inconvenience, the exposure to wind and rain but they were going home and the paddle-steamers could charge what they liked. For passengers had to show a profit in just the same way as the cargo did. The captain didn't care a toss for the passengers. He provided food as part of the deal, but what kind of food the passengers would find out only when they were on their journey and all you could do in protest was jump overboard and swim ashore and wait for the next boat which might not be so comfortable or watertight.

Saul felt the deck shudder and after one last long blast, the paddles on either side of the boat turned, grunting and grinding and gradually picking up speed. They were well out into the river when Saul saw Theodore Lang running along the levee shaking his fist and shouting. The words were lost on the breeze. Saul grinned and waved his hat over his head. He saw Lang grab for his gun and fire a salvo towards the moving boat. There was the sound of angry bees in the rigging, but they were out of range and swinging away into the middle of the channel. They were on their way.

TWO

Saul watched the ugly squat town that had grown up outside the fort grow gradually smaller as the paddle-steamer got under way. The levee was busy, for keelboats and mackinaws were unloading short-haul stores for the ever-changing community and the army which controlled the territory.

He felt a sense of relief. Not because he'd got away in time from Theodore Lang, for he was a greedy bastard who could well afford to be conned, but that he'd freed himself from three years of greed and toil up in the Montana gold-fields.

It was true he was no gold-miner. He had taken the gold from the miners relying on his wits and it had paid off. His heavy saddle-bags bore witness to that.

The *Star of the West* was an old steamer, battered by the Old Muddy, as the Missouri River

17

was called affectionately by the old-timers. She'd faced up to anything that the river in its evil temper could throw at her. Whitewater rapids, hidden rocks and tree stumps, sudden floods teeming from tributaries pouring water from the Rockies themselves never fazed the old girl. Her paddles lumbered on as did her old engines powered by cords of wood that sweating firemen threw into her greedy firebox.

She was flatbottomed and wide, barely taking in a six-foot draught and could slide over hidden rocks or navigate sandbanks in a remarkable way. There was a rapport between her and her skipper. Old Captain Short could tell by the beat of her heart in how many fathoms she wallowed.

The lower deck held the cargo and the passengers who couldn't afford the top deck. Those passengers made do with where they could find a bed, usually between the stinking bales of furs and hides. There was a railed-off area for horses with straps for their bellies to keep them upright in rough weather. That was where Saul slept, his saddle-bags hidden in the rough manger under a stack of hay which the captain had thoughtfully provided at a price that could have been a king's ransom.

There were several families aboard. Saul had seen several children peering over the white-painted rails to the deck below.

He'd also seen several women hustling the children away. One in particular caught his eye, a pretty dark-haired miss wearing a fetching blue bonnet who couldn't possibly have been anyone's mother.

He turned away from the rail when the river took a bend and Fort Benton was lost to view. The land on each side of the river was flat with the mountains showing blue-grey in the distance. All trees by the river had been cut down and used for fuel. Now it was silt, marshy and treacherous. At this time the river ran shallow with whitewater ripples lapping over rocks and boulders. The middle channel was the deepest and that was where the steamer carefully negotiated with a man on watch for ever-shifting sandbanks and dead trees that had been washed downriver during winter floods.

Twice on the journey down to Cook's Camp where they stopped to take on more wood, they had to backpaddle to ease off newly formed sandbanks.

There, Saul leaned over the rails and watched the upper passengers leave the steamboat to stretch their legs and allow the five children aboard to run and scream and play tag. He himself never left his mare alone, or that which he guarded with a pistol in an underarm holster.

He was wearing the red flannel undershirt and

drawers of the miner, underneath loose canvas pants, check shirt and buckskin jacket that marked him as a prospector of some kind. He merged into the crowd of miscellaneous itinerants that were fortune hunters, gamblers, land-grabbers and roustabouts, all going back to St Louis for one reason or another. Some were going back triumphant; some, broken in spirit if not in body.

There were others who preyed on the weak.

The girl he admired came aboard helping a frail lady who must have been her mother for they looked alike, but the girl was taller and stronger with an air about her which told him she had the strength of will to look after her mother and her younger brother and sister.

'Sarah! Watch Robert, while I help Mama to the top deck,' she called with all a schoolmarm's authority.

'Yes, Amy,' the child called dutifully, and then giggled as she caught the small boy by the scruff of the neck. 'Now watch yourself, Robert, or I'll push you overboard!'

There was a scuffle and Amy left her mother and boxed both children's ears. Then the older lady dropped her parasol and Saul saw his chance. Swiftly he darted forward and picked it up and returned it with a courtly bow he'd learned in one of the saloons back East.

The lady looked a little frightened, for Saul's face now sported a couple of days growth of beard and he hadn't washed or changed his clothes since coming aboard.

'Why, thank you, sir. You're very kind,' the light rather weak voice quavered.

'Glad to be of service, ma'am.' She gave him a tentative smile. 'Are you and your family going all the way to St Louis?'

Her face clouded and for a moment he thought she was going to cry.

'Yes. Unfortunately my husband is not with us. He ...' – she bit her lip, then raised her chin courageously – 'is no longer with us. Mr Grainger was shot by the Sioux.' She groped for a handkerchief.

'I'm sorry, ma'am. If there's anything I can do to help. ...'

She looked helplessly at him.

'Oh, there's no need. My daughter ... she is a very resolute girl. Takes after her father. Thank you, indeed.' She smiled again and blinked away the threatening tears.

'Mama! Are you ready to go up on top deck?' Amy Grainger was looking at him as if there was a bad smell under her nose.

'Amy, dear, this is Mr ... er ... I don't know your name, sir.'

Saul bowed again to both ladies.

'Saul Rhymer, at your service. It's been a pleasure, ma'am.'

Amy Grainger gave an audible sniff and Mrs Grainger said hastily, 'Mr Rhymer rescued my parasol. You know how clumsy I am. He was very kind.'

Saul got the distinct impression that the lady was a little overawed by her daughter, bullied in fact.

'Indeed? Well, I must thank you on my mother's behalf. Now come, Mama, God knows what mischief those children are getting into.' Without a backward glance she ushered her mother away.

Saul raised his eyebrows and turned down the corners of his mouth. Arrogant bitch! His eye caught an amused glance from one of the lower-deck passengers who had bedded down alongside a frisky young gelding with stout legs and a pack mule which the fellow had not unloaded.

'Give you the brush-off, didn't she? A fair lively filly that one and unbroken. I wouldn't mind teaching her a few tricks!'

Saul shrugged. 'A pretty enough wench but too mouthy for me.'

'Cold too. She'd ice up a feller's bed,' the man guffawed. Saul had to smile. His voice was loud when he agreed and gave his verdict.

'Yeh, a feller would have to be bribed with a

gold-mine to take her on. She's a born spinster!'

Suddenly from the deck above came the swoosh of water flung from a bucket. Both men jumped and cursed and Saul was drenched.

'What the hell. . . ?'

He looked upwards and saw a furious face, reddening with anger or something else, looking down at him.

'I'm sorry, Mr Rhymer, I didn't realize you were down below.' She gave him a frosty smile. 'You're lucky it was washing water and not the contents of the chamber pot!'

Then she flounced away and left Saul to strip to his waist and hang his wet clothes over the deck rails to dry.

'She heard that, y'know. Maybe she's not so cold, eh?' The little man looked at him with a grin. 'By the way, I'm known as Potman.' He stuck out his fist. They shook hands.' You're known as the Chiseller, aren't you? I've heard the men talk about you.'

Saul grinned. 'My fame goes before me!'

'I wish I had your luck. I'd show more than just a packhorse with bits and pieces to show for a stint up in the goldfields. Hurt me back and couldn't dig, so I fetched and carried for the others. Became a drummer selling spades and frypans and coffeepots for a storeman. It was no way to live, especially in the winter.'

'What will you do when you get down to St Louis?'

'Start again. Try and get on with a cattle outfit. There's still plenty of work for good cowpokes.'

'You're a bit small for a cowpoke.'

'Yeh, well, I generally end up as a cook. I'm good with a frypan and I make good doughballs.'

'That's useful. How about you and me teaming up together? You watch my back and I'll watch yours. We gotta long way to go before we hit St Louis.'

Potman grinned. 'I was hoping you'd come up with an idea like that. Two's better than one when it comes to a journey like this. D'you reckon this captain knows what he's doing?'

'Captain Short? I dunno about him but he's got a good pilot aboard. I reckon we won't have too many mishaps on the way.'

'It all depends on how long it takes. If we get bogged down before winter sets in, then it could be lethal, especially for those women and children up there on that top deck.'

Saul looked thoughtful. He looked up at the upper deck and then at the wheelhouse above that. He could just see the captain and his pilot through the dirty glass of the window. Give them a few days and he was going to be up there assessing things for himself. He'd heard the captain was a heavy drinker, but he wasn't for frightening his new partner.

It was time to mingle with the other passengers and assess them. Put them in categories; the potential gamblers, the conmen, the hard-assed miners who punched first and asked questions afterwards. They were all there and all had one thing in common; they were survivors and had the muscles to prove it.

He made his mind up fast. If Potman was to be his partner then he must trust him.

'You stay here and watch the horses. There's a swell on, so watch their legs.'

'What are you going to do?' Potman watched him curiously.

'Going to assess the enemy. Everyone's an enemy until you know otherwise.'

'You mean to start a card school?'

'Why not? They're going to get bored before we get to St Louis. They can't drink forever. They've got to have some excitement, especially the miners.'

'Goddammit! I wish I played cards! But I've never had a head for it. Can't add up to more than five. I'll never make me a stake!'

'Don't worry, Potman. You watch the horses and my back and I'll make us both a stake.'

'You mean you haven't made yourself a stake out in them goldfields?'

Saul hesitated. He trusted Potman up to a point, but he wasn't going to admit that he had a stash aboard.

'Not exactly. Enough to get me a start in St
Louis, if I don't lose it all from now till then!'

'Caw!' Potman marvelled.

'Why in hell are you going back, if you haven't
made your pile?'

'Same reason as you. Sick to death of pigging it
and I don't fancy another winter up in them hills.
I've seen men with frostbite and it wasn't only
feet and fingers! No sir! I'm going back before I
turn into an old man.'

Saul made his casual way along the over-
crowded lower deck. His broad naked back,
bronzed and all rippling muscle made him stand
out in the crowd of passengers. Mentally he
counted as he elbowed his way through the
throng.

They all smelt and the stink from the furs and
buffalo hides seemed to surround the old
paddle-steamer like a fog. The river stank also
and it was like steaming through soup. Its
yellow-brown water hid the uncharted depths
and a lookout in the stern of the boat called out
the fathoms as slowly they moved along the
channel.

There was also the smell of woodsmoke which
belched from two iron funnels that heated the old
boilers and brought up the pressure of steam and
turned the clumsy wooden paddles. There was the
constant churning of creamy foaming water on

each side of the boat as they passed along the waterway.

He spoke to several men as he passed. He wasn't for joining anyone at this time. All he wanted was to gauge the opposition. He knew the time would come when someone would approach him. He mustn't appear too keen. That way could betray just how successful he'd been up in the goldfields.

Then, quietly, he mounted the stairs to the upper deck. He might as well take stock of any other gamblers on the prod.

His eye lit on a man he'd known in Bear Gulch. Damn! He'd been present when he'd done the old gold-mine scam up in the hills. He held his breath as the man looked him over, but there was no sign of recognition, which was understandable as Saul had worn his regular gambling gear of white shirt, fancy waistcoat and long black frockcoat, which regretfully he'd left behind in his hasty exit from Fort Benton.

The man nodded. He was leaning over the rail smoking a cigar. He half-smiled and raised the cigar.

'Little woman hates the smell. I gotta stay out of the cabin until the stink disappears, she says. Women! She should get her nose out here. This damn river smells much worse!'

'Yea. I suppose we'll get used to it before we get to St Louis.'

'Ah, you're going all the way? We're getting off at Bismarck and damned glad. She's grumbling already at the lack of facilities. It's her own fault. She insisted on coming with me. Didn't trust me, y'know. A great little woman, but with a suspicious mind.' He sighed. 'Can't have me a decent drink or a hand of cards. She's got me hogtied!'

Saul grinned. 'You'll get over it, sir. Marriage has its compensations.' He moved on and saw that all ten cabins were occupied by families or top-brass soldiers. There was plenty of deck room for exercise. He also noted the well-polished brass cannon on the foredeck facing the riverbank, a silent reminder of Indian and guerrilla attacks that, when they came, usually happened when the steamer pulled in at night alongside a woodyard for refuelling. The woodyards were built like forts with high wooden palisades surrounded by flat country devoid of trees with only stumps left to show that it had once been forest.

The further the woodsmen had to travel to haul in the tree trunks to saw into logs and the risk of Indian attack made the cords of logs more expensive for the steamer captains.

Sometimes the woodyards were deserted after Indian raids and then the steamer would lose time while the whole crew would forage for wood for the ever-greedy firebox. Those were the times when the captain cursed and even passengers had to work all night to get the woodpiles stacked on board, so that the journey could commence again.

There was no sympathy for or curiosity of the fate of what were commonly known as the 'wood-hawks'. They were a scurvy bunch of knaves at the best of times and would cheat a captain on the amount of wood in a cord if he appeared inexperienced. It was all a matter of survival and beat the river, keep the steam up and the boilers from bursting.

Saul saw no sign of the Graingers and after a few polite observations to an army colonel, two captains and four subalterns who were going on home leave, descended again to the lower deck. It looked as if it was going to be a boring journey.

Potman was snoring when he returned, his mouth open and blasting out a stench that could have come out of a sewer. Saul looked at him with distaste and then kicked him in the ribs.

'Hey! Wake up. What the hell you doing sleeping on the job?'

Potman looked up at him and frowned.

'We got nothing to steal, pal, or at least I haven't. Nobody's going to ride off with the horses, not unless they jump overboard so what's your beef?'

Saul shrugged. He'd have to be careful or this little weasel might guess, and if he was curious he'd start looking. . . . He'd have to find a new place to stash his saddle-bags. He cursed the gold. It wasn't something you could hide easy on board. But if the faintest sniff of gold was suspected, then all hell would break loose. He would have to get his wits working.

'I'm going down to the galley,' he said abruptly. 'They'll be dishing out the rations soon. It'll be pickled pork and bread as usual I expect. I'm gonna have word with Captain Short about hunting up some fresh meat if we sight a herd anywhere near the water.'

'You'll think he'll stop?'

'Why not? The bastard must be sick of pickled pork like we all are. The best grub's kept for the cabin passengers even though we're paying through the nose for passage.'

'Yeah, well, we're just the roughnecks down on this deck. We're not supposed to need a bit of comfort.' Potman grinned showing gaps between his teeth. 'Maybe you can give him a bit of blarney and get us some decent grub especially if you offer to keep the stewpot full.'

There were large barrels and small kegs as well as bales stacked amidships, all tangled with ropes, and a couple of large wooden chests cleated to the deck. He wondered what was inside and reckoned it must be guns and ammunition to be dished out during an emergency. The conclusion made him feel easier. Captain Short evidently was doing all he could to defend his ship.

The galley cook was broad-shouldered with a paunch like a beer barrel and whiskers that could have hidden a bird's nest. He was standing with a huge cleaver in his hand when Saul clattered down the wooden stairs and bent to enter the galley.

There was a faint judder as the boat steamed over the shallows taking in little draught and the paddles groaned and churned the water into a heaving mass. The thump of the engines came clearly. The cook cursed as wood in his stove jumped and rattled, and water in a black iron pan slopped and caused a hissing of steam.

'What you want? No passengers to come into the galley. There's a notice outside. Can't you read?' He pointed the knife at Saul's chest. Saul put his hands shoulder high.

'No offence, pal. Just wondered about the rations.'

'You'll get 'em when they're ready,' grunted the cook. 'I'm busy fixing the cabin passengers' grub. They're a nit-picking lot, all right.' He sighed. 'I don't hold with women aboard. They expect a real cook. I'm only a cattle-trail cookie with experience of a chuck wagon and if they don't like it, they can do the other thing!'

'I was going to ask the captain about doing a bit

of hunting if we see any game.' The man stared at him and then guffawed deep in his stomach. Saul frowned. 'What's so funny?'

'We're coming into Sioux country and they don't take kindly to us white folk hunting in their territory.'

'They'd never know if the herd was down drinking at the river.'

'Oh, they'll know all right. That's why we stick to pork and dried beef. The bastards are there even if you don't see them. They follow all the riverboats up and downstream, watching and waiting.'

'Waiting for what?'

'For a steamer to run aground on one of them sandbars. Those goddamn bars shift endlessly with the wind and flow of the water. The Sioux get in there before the boats get silted up, if they get the chance, and loot the cargo and anything else they can lift. I've seen steamers look like skeletons with their bones picked clean.'

'What about the crews?'

The cook put a finger across his throat.

'If the swine catch you, you've had it. Mind you, Captain Short's been through a few sorties. He's well known amongst the Indians. Keeps a few gewgaws to give 'em as goodwill like. They know he carries a useful arsenal and is not afraid to use it.'

32

'So that's what those big chests hold up on deck?'

'Yeah, we got enough ammunition to rout 'em and the captain keeps a trunkful of dynamite up in his cabin. One stick slung at 'em usually shifts 'em.'

'So we might get away with some hunting?'

'You might if you're fool enough. You'll have to ask the captain. If you can pull it off, there'll be good rations for you, on the quiet like.' They grinned at each other and Saul made his way up on deck.

He had a lot to think about.

He'd been conscious for some time of the faint throb of engine and paddles which was now growing stronger and then came the blast of a steamer coming up around a wide bend in the river towards them. Its hooter was sending out two-minute warnings and the entire ship's crew and passengers lined both decks as the white-painted *Amarylis* came chugging into view. There were cheers and waves from all sides and both steamers lost way as the captains bawled across the water at each other.

'Ho, there, *Star of the West*,' came a stentorian voice. 'How she be further up the river?'

'All quiet and shipshape. Water rising but steady as she goes. Sandbanks negotiable.'

'Thanks, Skipper. You watch out for wreckers

'bout fifty miles downstream. The woodyard's burnt out, so get your crew to take wood on board before you get there, or you'll have to steam another hundred and fifty miles. There's also a couple of boats grounded on sandbanks and the wreckers are around like flies in a honeypot. Prime your big gun, Skipper, and be ready.'

'Will do. Thanks for the warning, Captain.' The *Amarylis* sailed on, chugging and straining against the flow of the river, like the old dowager that she was.

The *Star of the West* gave three blasts on her hooter and soon they were round the bend of the river which widened with high banks and tall pines which grew right to the water's edge. The banks were too high for the trafficking boats to stop and refuel because of the danger of rip-tides and fast currents.

It was heart-wrenchingly beautiful country, but Saul was conscious of the savagery behind the beauty. To be lost in this wilderness meant death. A man would freeze to death in winter or die of thirst away from the river in summer. Then there were the hazards of hostile Indians and bands of outlaws that lived and preyed on the river traffic. For all the boats making a living up and down the river weren't large paddle-steamers; some were flat-bottomed boats that plied their trade from one town to the next, keelboats, wide mackinaws that four men could pole along the shallows, and bull boats, the frail coracles made from willow strips and the hide of a bull buffalo. They used bull hides because they leaked less than did the female hides They were capable of carrying vast weights of merchandise across the river itself at its narrowest, therefore gaining access to one side or the other.

That night the *Star of the West* pulled in beside a tributary of the river and though the crew grumbled, all knew that they had to get out and saw down the trees needed for the next stretch of water. The cash saved from buying direct from the woodhawks would be distributed amongst the crew.

The cabin passengers grumbled at the ceaseless sawing and crashing of trees which went on all night, and when someone complained to Captain Short, he lost his temper and roared that he didn't give a damn for the passengers' convenience and if the man in question was but half a man he'd volunteer to help out.

'You've got muscles! Get out there and use 'em! The sooner we get stocked up, the sooner we'll be on our way!'

Saul and some of the miners took the hint. The miners especially were used to solid hard work and they could burn up some of their utter boredom in fresh air and exercise. Soon, they were laughing and singing sea shanties as they took turns to saw up logs and haul them aboard in large nets hoisted by a rig, a couple of men turning the big wheel.

Saul was sweating, his muscles rippling and aching, but he felt such a sense of freedom and peace it was amazing. The scent of pine was strong as the trees came crashing down and, as he hacked at the small branches leaving the straight trunks ready for sawing, he felt that this was the life for him. It beat sitting pitting his wits at cards. It seemed that his whole life was nothing but a foggy dream and this was the reality.

He straightened his aching back and stretched, vague thoughts coming to him of starting a new kind of life when he reached St Louis. He would buy land and settle; maybe raise cattle and horses; marry. A vision of a womanly figure by his side tantalized him. He couldn't visualize that woman. Most of the women he'd known had been saloon women, or the dull wives of ranchers or city slickers who'd been trained by their husbands to fetch and carry and not think for themselves.

He could never settle for that kind of woman. Nor the other kind who'd strip off for any man if the price was right.

That left a girl like Miss High and Mighty Grainger, and though she was attractive to him, he wouldn't touch her with a pole. Her tongue would have to be cut out first!

He grinned as he wiped sweat from his forehead and took a better grip on the axe and went to work again with a vicious swing. The future would have to look after itself.

They were hauling in the last load of wood when the wreckers came howling along the riverbank, firing shots, led by a formidable giant of a man with a black eyepatch, blasting away with an ancient shotgun.

The men still on the riverbank panicked and jumped into the shallow water and stumbled or fell as they made for the steamer.

There were yells and shouts from both sides and Captain Short frantically tried to open his cache of arms. But two of his crew were hit before the male passengers knew what had happened and could scramble into their clothes and find their weapons.

Saul raced up to the top deck, seeing Amy poking her head out of the Grainger cabin to see what all the row was about.

'Get inside and stay there!' he shouted. 'We're being attacked by outlaws.' She gasped, but said nothing and slammed her door. Saul rushed on up to the wheelhouse outside of which stood the brass cannon.

He could see the captain on the lower deck

doling out guns and ammunition to the crew and those passengers who didn't carry weapons. There was a cacophony of sound amidst screams and shouts from passengers and invaders alike.

'We want the gold,' bawled the man with the eyepatch as he swarmed up the wooden struts of the vessel.

Saul eyed the cannon. He knew it was at the ready at all times. It was now up to him as he saw the soldiers on the lower deck firing in a disciplined way and causing havoc to the oncoming cut-throats.

Saul looked about him and found the tinderbox and remembered what the soldiers at Fort Benton had done on the occasion of the old commander's funeral when they'd given him a good send off. Thank God he'd been nosy enough to watch!

He found the cotton waste and the plunger, set it alight and rammed it home, then pulled the lanyard and jumped back as the little cannon exploded and leapt into the air as it spouted iron rivets and balls down on to the riverbank below.

Then it was as if the whole world turned red. Dawn broke over the hills and the first rays of the sun showed the carnage of mangled bodies, twisted branches of trees and blood everywhere.

Saul wanted to be sick.

A great cheer went up from the passengers and crew below and then came the grim mopping up of the men who'd gotten aboard. One of the subalterns had shot Mr Eyepatch in the throat and with the leader dead, those still alive jumped overboard and splashed ashore, bullets sending them on their way.

But there were casualties on both sides. Captain Short counted four passengers dead and two crewmen and more than twenty wounded. The invaders had come off the worst. There were five on board killed outright and many more on the riverbank.

It was full daylight before the steamer got underway, for the graves had to be dug and prayers said over the unfortunate ones while the womenfolk patched up the wounded.

The outlaws they left to rot or to the mercy of those who'd been left alive.

Saul felt a sense of relief when the engines throbbed into life and the steam built up and the paddles began to turn. He hoped their next port of call would not be so hazardous.

THREE

Saul leant against the rail of the upper deck behind the cluster of men listening to Captain Short. He saw that the lower-deck passengers were well represented at this meeting. They could all be described as leaders, representing the trappers, the traders and, the most prevalent, those successful gold-miners going home with their payload.

It was they who had insisted on this meeting. They wanted to know what Captain Short had planned for any more attacks by roughneck outlaws, hostile Indians or wreckers.

'We want no more fiascos like this last one, Captain. You were warned there might be trouble and yet you didn't set a watch.' The man raised his fist into the air.

'Because all hands were hauling wood,' bellowed back the captain. 'I didn't reckon on the bastards coming upstream. I figured we should

41

sail right past them.' Captain Short breathed heavily with temper. 'Goddammit! I haven't a crystal ball! I don't predict the future.'

Saul watched the man who was spouting his mouth off. He'd seen him laying down the law with the lower-deck passengers and reckoned he thought himself cock of the midden. Now the man swung round to the others.

'Who amongst you is carrying gold?' His eyes raked the faces looking up at him. Saul kept his hand down. Like hell would he admit to carrying gold dust!

He watched the hands rise and was startled at the number, and they were only the ones representing the rest of the passengers. This boat could be carrying over a million dollars in gold!

It was an intriguing thought.

It could be disastrous for the *Star of the West*, if a hint of it got beyond the boat itself. Saul's blood ran cold at the thought.

They'd have every roughneck plying the Missouri River after them.

Suddenly he made his mind up and stepped forward.

'Gentlemen, as I see it, we must arrange guard duty for every man aboard ship so that it is manned twenty-four hours a day.'

'But why should we?' a well-dressed passenger howled. 'I carry no gold. I'm a trader from

Jefferson City. I carry nothing that would be valuable for pirates.'

'You could lose your life,' Saul shouted grimly. 'All of you; and the women and children could lose their lives if this boat was set on fire!'

There were deafening shouts of agreement from some and dissent from others.

'I'm a bachelor,' shouted a thin, bald-headed fellow. 'I'm a clerk not a gunman. I don't see why I should risk my life for someone else's gold!'

'Then you'd better get off my boat at the next port of call,' roared the captain. 'If we're to do this properly, everyone must pull his weight. I propose letting the colonel here organize this as a military operation. That way I can sanction the use of arms. I'm willing to empty my lockers of weapons to be used by those defending our ship!'

'Hear, hear! Well said!' came the cry from all sides and so it was that Colonel Jason and the two captains took command, much to the chagrin of the leader of the lower deck.

'What about the gold? It should be registered and stowed below deck,' the man shouted, 'instead of every man defending his own property. The steamship company should be responsible for its safety.'

'That's up to the individual,' answered the captain quickly. 'Why are you so interested in having all the gold aboard in one place, sir? Answer me that.'

'Why, for the good of all these brave miners who've sweated blood to get themselves a stake! It would be easier to defend if it was all in one place. That's logical, isn't it?'

'You're mighty caring, mister. Are you prepared to release your gold into my care?'

The man laughed and hesitated.

'I have no gold, Captain. I merely offer the suggestion for others.'

'Then shut your mouth!'

Suddenly there was a scuffle and before the stunned passengers could react, the captain was reeling back from a blow to his belly. He hit one of the stanchions and came back swinging his arms like a gorilla and charged the disgruntled passenger with a flying headbutt.

'I'm captain here and I don't take crap from anyone!' He grabbed the man's flailing arm and twisted savagely and, before the passengers could make way, the man was catapulted over the side and plunged down into the shallow water of the Missouri.

The captain leaned over the rail, clenching it with both hands.

'I hope you hit a rock, you bastard! Come back aboard when you've cooled off and the next time you try that trick I'll clap you in irons!'

The man spluttered and cursed, shaking himself like a wet dog to the laughter and catcalls of the watching passengers.

'Serve the swine right,' muttered someone standing beside Saul. 'He's a troublemaker that one.'

'Do you know him?' asked Saul.

'Yeah. He was a supervisor for the St Louis Mining Company, but he had sticky fingers. Charlie Breckon is his name and he's lying when he says he has no gold. I wouldn't trust him with my ma's gold teeth!'

'A bad hat, eh?'

'Yeah, with a long memory for grudges. Captain Short will have to have eyes in his butt!'

'Like that, is he? Now I wonder why he was insisting on all gold on board being stashed together?'

'God knows. Like I said, man, he's crooked all right. Maybe he's set up a deal to be clinched at some prearranged landing site; who knows?'

Saul was thoughtful and watched the man climb aboard at a distance. He wondered whether he was a cardplayer. It might be interesting to get to know Mr Charles Breckon better.

He went to look for Potman but on the way one of the roustabouts stopped him.

'The captain would like to see you in the wheel-house when you have time.'

Saul laughed. 'I've all the time in the world, mister. I'll go now.' As he made his way up to the upper bridge and wheelhouse, he wondered what the captain could see fit to talk to him about.

The captain greeted him heartily and held out his hand.

'Ah, Mr Rhymer, glad to see you. Will you sit down?'

They were in Captain Short's small cabin attached to the wheelhouse. It was more of an office than actual living-quarters. There were hooks for clothes and a hammock, but the rest was given over to survey maps of the river, plotting gear and huge piles of cargo manifests. Saul wondered how he could find anything specific in a hurry.

He did notice the chest that presumably held the dynamite and the clumsy safe and, in a rack above the hammock, a couple of well-oiled shotguns and a handgun.

Captain Short saw him looking at his armoury.

'Mostly for show. I keep 'em handy for mutiny and the odd passenger who needs restraining. We get some very queer characters on board. One feller thought he was General Robert E. Lee and wanted to take over my boat! He got short shrift I can tell you! We threw him overboard!'

'I don't think, Captain, that you sent for me to talk about crazy passengers. What is it you want?'

The captain reached down into a locker and brought up two far from clean glasses and a half-empty bottle of whiskey.

'Here, have a snort while I tell you.' He poured two stiff measures. Then, lifting his own in a toast, he drained half of it. 'I've been watching you, Mr Rhymer. I saw the way you used yourself during that last little run-in. Your reputation didn't do you justice, Mr Rhymer. I thought you would be a troublemaker aboard.'

'And?'

'Now I think differently.'

'You want my help? It's the gold situation, isn't it?'

The captain nodded and emptied his glass.

'I don't know who I can trust; not that Breckon feller for one and as for the army officers, you can't always trust them to do the right thing. The colonel might be relied upon but the others seem too young and green and I daresay didn't see action during the war. To my mind they're new recruits just getting broken in.'

'What are you saying, Captain?'

'You didn't lose your head in a crisis. Let's face it, Mr Rhymer, we've nearly two thousand miles of river to negotiate before we get to St Louis and there's going to be comings and goings at each major township on the way. I would like you to get to know those lower-deck passengers and pick out a nice round number who're going all the way and turn yourselves into a fighting unit. What d'you say?'

Saul hesitated. Then, 'You really think we're in danger because of the gold aboard?'

Captain Short shrugged.

'This was the last steamer leaving Fort Benton with miners leaving the goldfields before the winter sets in. It stands to reason someone will figure it out that most of my passengers will be loaded. It's happened before, mister. It'll happen again.'

Saul whistled quietly through his teeth.

'If I can form a security guard, do we get paid by the company?'

The captain looked uncomfortable.

'This is off the record. It's your own lives you'll be defending. I've got twenty-five rifles locked up in that chest down below and the ammo to go with them. Twelve for my crew and the rest for you and your men. I'd be mighty relieved if I knew I had extra men to rely on.'

'Well, if you put it that way, I can't refuse. I guess my life is worth that much! I'll see what I can do.'

They shook hands.

'Oh, by the way, don't mention this to the military. The colonel might be a bit touchy about this undercover stuff.'

Saul gave a wry grin.

'They look good in uniform on parade, but not for fending off shipboard attacks! I noticed a couple of the subalterns were a bit green when we came through the last lot of rapids!'

'And they were a doddle to what we'll be up against before we get to Sioux City! Half the passengers will be laid low then! Are you a good sailor, Mr Rhymer?'

'Yeah, you might say so. Mind you I've never rafted over whitewater, but I don't suppose I ever will!'

'Good. Make sure the men you choose have strong guts. Hostiles, wreckers and pirates often lie in wait for that part of the river which knocks hell out of paddle-steamers. Trouble is, the river is always changing course because of the silt washed downriver during storms.'

'How many times have you battled the river, Captain?'

'I've been up and down the Missouri ever since I was a boy in short britches. I know it as well as any man living who can read the temper of the beast, for it's a goddamn treacherous, mean beast that holds no quarter for any living thing. Yes, sir! You treat it with respect or it'll get you in the end!'

Saul took his time surveying his fellow passengers and chose his men carefully. The loudmouth brash brawlers he passed over. They were the ones who'd brought liquor aboard and couldn't be trusted. He chose hard-bitten miners used to deprivation, with muscles of iron and the will to defend the gold they'd sweated months and years to wrest from the unforgiving earth.

He also recruited a dozen trappers whose bales of fur, and hides the boat carried. They had their own weapons so were a bonus.

And they were all survivors.

Soon, he could report that the men were now willing to do two-hour shifts for twenty-four hours a day and the captain gave permission for them to have two lookouts on the top deck next to the wheelhouse and behind the captain's small cabin.

As the steamer slowly paddled her way down-stream, stopping at intervals for refuelling, Saul felt a lot easier in his mind. Never again would they be caught napping. The steamer's rifles and ammunition were not distributed amongst the lower-deck passengers and the rich families and the military boys were left in ignorance. It was better that way.

It was getting to be a boring journey and many card schools were set up along with crap games, bird-shooting contests where much ammunition, especially from the first-class passengers, was wasted.

The captain organized prayer meetings and choir singing, mainly to keep the womenfolk

happy and a crewman was ordered to entertain
the children by teaching them knots and to dance
the hornpipe to the jigging lilt of a single penny
whistle that his mate provided.

They passed the Musselshell rivermouth without incident and docked at Forts Peck and Copelin
where the ladies could stretch their legs while the
galley cook took on more pickled pork and dry
staples, compliments of the military, Colonel
Jason being an old buddy of the commander of
Fort Copelin. So he was of some use after all,
thought Saul sourly. The good colonel had spent
most of his time fussing round the ladies and Amy
Grainger, in particular, which had sent Saul into
a rage when he'd seen them laughing together.

The dirty old bastard was at least twenty years
older than Amy. Every time he saw him he wanted
to smash in his face.

There had been a nasty incident when they'd
left the Wolf Creek Indian Agency and a warband
of the Sioux had made a half-hearted attack on
the boat when it had become stuck on a sandbank. Chief Uglala was unhappy at the tribe's
treatment at the hands of the Indian Agent who
was authorized by the government to pay them a
levy every six months of food and blankets, but
the agent had been keeping back part of the
consignment for himself and then selling it to
other Sioux tribes at inflated prices. It was

enough to start a little war, but the brass cannon and the prompt action of Saul's guards sent them on their way.

The next problem was lightening the loads aboard the steamer to float her off a hidden sandbank. Under protest, the cargo was manhandled ashore and all hands poled and sweated to 'grasshopper' her into deeper water.

This grasshopper business was new to Saul and he watched, fascinated, while the crew used long pine poles to lever her and slide her over correctly positioned poles until she belly-flopped into a splurge of whitewater, her paddles whirring madly as the steam sent her forward while firemen and engineers sweated below deck.

A cheer went up from the passengers who'd chosen to go ashore and watch the procedure. Then began the hauling aboard of the cargo and the *Star of the West* continued her journey.

They shot the rapids before they came to the mouth of the Yellowstone River. It was a white-knuckle ride as the pilot and the captain watched for hidden rocks and manoeuvred the boat into a safe channel. The roar of the water pounded their ears and when they finally sailed into calmer water the silence was intense.

Amy came to Saul, standing at the rail. He looked at her.

'You all right? How did your mother cope?'

She nodded. Her face looked drawn and tired.

'She's sick. She worries too much. I wish my father was here. She hasn't got over his death.'

'I'm sorry. You've got a lot of responsibility, what with the children and all.'

'I'm afraid and I've never been afraid in my life before.'

The usually strong voice cracked with strain. He covered the hand resting on the rail with his.

'Look, Amy, this isn't the time to talk about you and me, but I want you to know that if anything bad happens, you can rely on me.'

Her lips quivered. 'Thank you.' Then she sighed. 'You'll never know how I've longed to have someone I can lean on. My father was a doctor, you know, and we all leant on him. He was so strong. I still can't believe I'll never see him again.'

'What happened?'

'He was coming back from seeing a patient and he got shot in the crossfire between settlers and raiders. My mother's family is in St Louis. We decided it was right for the children's sake to go back there. Sometimes I doubt if my mother will ever see her sisters.' She gave a watery smile. 'But there is no need for me to burden you with my fears. What is to be will be. That was my father's maxim and I believe it.'

Saul was stirred. He'd never felt so emotionally

for any woman in his life. Oh yes, there had been moments when his flesh had been stirred, but not in this new way. He thought back to his previous life. He'd been a selfish bastard. He and he alone had been the one to worry about. Now, he looked at this strong, capable girl with the schoolmarm air, whom he'd taken a dislike to because of her arrogant big mouth, and saw a new image of her as being just a frightened young thing with too much responsibility on her slender shoulders.

He wanted to put his arms about her and protect her and was aware that she was unknowingly casting a snare over him that would change his life forever, whether they were together or not.

'Amy, I love you,' he said impulsively, 'but this is not the time to talk of that or whether you could love me. But rest assured, I'm there for you at any time you need me. Right?'

She blinked and wiped her eyes with the back of her hand, then sniffed and reached up and kissed his cheek.

'You're very kind.' Then without a backward glance she slipped away and he watched as she returned to their cabin. He sighed. God knows what the future held. They still had more than a thousand miles to travel before they came to St Louis, and every mile could spell danger either by the river itself or the human marauders who infested its banks.

If anxiety hadn't dogged their passage so that every waking moment was taken up watching the riverbanks, the changing terrain they passed through would have been an experience never forgotten. Great mountain ranges, often blue-black, or grey tinged with purple, or topped with white, glistening ice, rose high above pine forests that seemed to go on forever. In between there were arid rocky plains that held their own ochre and pink beauty as they swept past on that downward journey.

Then there were the birds, and the herds of horses and buffalo glimpsed after the rolling, buffeting sound of many feet pounding the earth.

Twice the steamer anchored in midstream while the trappers and Saul went after the buffalo and brought back meat that would last the whole ship for at least two weeks.

Saul and Potman had taken their horses ashore and led the chase, manoeuvring the chosen buffalo into the path of the shootists who blazed away with shotguns and rifles. You didn't have to be a good marksman to bring a beast down. They were as thick as flies on a corpse.

It did the horses good. Stretched their legs and pepped them up and worked off some of the corn they ate on the journey.

Saul was beginning to relax. Maybe Captain Short was being a worrity old woman. Perhaps the gold aboard was still a secret and they would reach St Louis without further danger.

Without knowing it, all the guards relaxed. Some of them forgot to show up for guard duty. Some showed up and found a corner behind the captain's cabin and settled down for a snooze during the night hours. Saul himself was coming to regard this as a time when he could advance his courtship.

He had his first quarrel with Amy when he tackled her about Colonel Jason.

'Arnold? He's a very nice man and humorous; he makes me laugh. Your idea that he is courting me is preposterous! Why, he's old enough to be my father!'

'He doesn't look on you as his daughter! Has he tried to kiss you?' She stared at him and then slapped his cheek.

'How dare you! You're revolting!'

'Revolting, am I?' He caught her by her forearms and pulled her close. He could feel the beating of her heart. 'Goddammit, Amy, I don't want you even talking to the man! It's not talking anyway, it's flirting!' She struggled to free herself, furious and indignant.

'Take your hands off me! I'm *not* a flirt!'

Then he kissed her hard and she slapped his cheek with more force this time. It stung.

'Leave me alone! In future if I need help, I'll ask the colonel!'

'You do just that,' he said between clenched teeth, and stalked away to find Potman who was lying snoring beside the horses. He kicked him viciously in the ribs, making the poor fellow blink and scramble to his feet.

'What . . . what's happened? Are we being attacked?'

'No. Just don't sleep on the job. You're supposed to be watching the horses. You don't want one of them to break a leg when we hit a shoal, do you?'

Potman rubbed his ribs. By, that Saul was a funny swine! He watched as Saul kicked one of the stall's uprights in temper. He wondered who or what had upset him. He couldn't understand Saul, but for all that he was glad he was his friend.

Potman had never had many friends he could trust in his life until now. He wasn't going to complain because of a kick between his ribs. It was a small price to pay for the gambler's protection.

FOUR

Saul watched the impassive face carefully and saw the faint flicker of the eyelids. So Charlie Breckon was beginning to worry, Charlie Breckon was a bad loser. Over the weeks, Saul had been studying the fellow. There was something about him that irked Saul. It was as if Charlie Breckon was savouring a joke no one else could share. His manner was mocking, cocksure, and the only time his composure slipped was when he lost at cards.

The stakes weren't high. None of the miners on board would play for high stakes. It had been too tough grinding out a small fortune for themselves in the goldfields for that and, as for the trappers, their real cash would come when the cargo was disposed of.

But even losing a few dollars made Charlie Breckon mean.

Suddenly he flung down his cards and leaned

forward so that he was eyeball to eyeball with a smiling Saul.

'If you can beat two kings and jacks, I'll know you're cheating!' he growled, and Saul quietly laid down his running flush of diamonds.

Charlie Breckon swore and, without warning, slammed a meaty fist into Saul's face who immediately somersaulted backwards from the bale of fur on which he was sitting.

He came up fighting and found Charlie Breckon crouched ready and waiting with a knife in his hand. Saul didn't waste time protesting his innocence for he had been cheating, but grabbed a grappling hook and, with a bound, lunged for the heavier man.

But Charlie Breckon was fitter than his thick body belied and he dodged as the hook caught and jammed in the woodwork.

Then he was on Saul and wielding the knife like a madman. Saul caught his wrist and twisted a foot around the big man's ankle. They teetered together and crashed to the ground. The watching men scattered to give them room on the deck.

Potman elbowed his way through the crowd to watch. He'd told Saul on many occasions to watch out for Breckon's temper, but Saul had laughed and said he could handle him. Then Saul would give Potman his half share of the night's take and Potman took pleasure in the fact that some of it had come out of Breckon's pocket.

He was ready to do battle for Saul. He couldn't watch his protector and sole means of income coming to a sticky end by some mean trick from a bastard like Breckon.

He waited and shouted with the rest as the battle first went one way and then the other. Twice Potman had raised the blacksmith's hammer he held at his side, ready to smash Breckon's skull like an eggshell, and twice he refrained, as Saul lunged and twisted and kicked Breckon around the deck.

Suddenly it was all over as Breckon caught a running kick in the crotch. With legs drawn together and head forward, he plummeted over the side of the boat and landed in the water behind the thrashing paddles. Potman looked over the side and saw the man bob up and start swimming. A pity he hadn't got entangled in the paddles, he thought sourly, and watched while some of Charlie's sycophantic pals pulled him aboard.

He found Saul squatting on a bale and leaning forward to get his breath back. Sweat, with blood from a cut to the head, dripped from him, but he was grinning.

'Here's the winnings: take your share and hold mine while I get a bucket of water and sluice myself down.'

'How much is there?'

'How the hell do I know? I haven't had time to count it.'

Potman was awed. Never in his life would he trust uncounted cash to another man or woman.

'You trust me that much?'

'Of course. We're pards, aren't we?' A hint of amusement showed in the puffed-up eyes. Then he staggered away to get a bucket from the galley to toss overboard on a rope and bring up some of the thick, silted water to sluice himself down.

He was just doing that, standing naked in the prow of the ship, hidden behind several squat wooden barrels, when Amy found him. Water streamed from his hard, muscled frame and the sting of it had given him new energy. He stood proud and tall.

He turned when he heard her gasp.

'Goddammit! What are you doing here?' He tried to cover himself up with a dirty towel he'd borrowed from the galley cook. He wasn't embarrassed about showing his body to a woman, but he was as sure as hell embarrassed at Amy seeing him. There was a lot of difference between Amy and a woman who was paid cash for her services.

He was angry that he felt that way.

'Get to hell out of it!' he shouted. 'You're not a strumpet. You shouldn't be here. It's not fitting!'

'I . . . heard about the fight. I thought you were

hurt.' She looked at the puffy eyes and the bruised skin of his shoulders and arms. 'You *are* hurt! I've seen naked men before. I can help you!'

'Not this naked, you haven't! Anyhow, your pa was there to make it respectable.'

'Respectable?' She started to laugh. 'My God, nobody thinks of respectability when there's patching-up to do! But if you're not seriously hurt and you don't need me, then I'll go.' She turned away.

'Wait, just a minute.' She turned back eagerly.

'Yes, what is it?'

He hesitated and then said quietly, 'I'm sorry I bawled you out. I didn't want you to see me like this. You were really worried about me?'

'Yes, of course I was.' She looked down unable to meet his eyes.

'Does that mean . . . you have some real feeling for me? That I can hope. . . ?'

She looked shyly at him and then smiled and it was like the sun breaking through after rain.

'I . . . guess so.' There was a catch in her voice.

'May I kiss you?'

'You kissed me before, but you didn't ask.'

'But that was different. I wanted to make a point.'

'And this time?'

'Is to show my feeling for you.' Then he looked down at himself. 'Maybe I should wait.' The towel betrayed a bulge. 'I'll claim my kiss later.' She smiled and stepped forward and put her arms about his bare shoulders.

'I'm rather tired of you taking charge and expecting me to obey you. I'll kiss you now.' Her cool lips sought and found his and then, as his arms closed about her, she dragged herself away, laughing.

Charlie Breckon came up spluttering and cursing as two of his cronies dragged him aboard.

'I'll kill the bastard! I'll have his. . . !' He shook himself like a half-drowned dog.

'Be quiet, you fool!' one of the men growled into his ear. 'You're lucky you didn't split your head wide open on those rocks below!'

Breckon looked down into the water and saw the water-smooth rocks that stood up like worn-down teeth that the boat was negotiating with the help of a navigator who was intoning with monotonous regularity, 'Four fathoms, mark you, and helm to the starboard, and 'ware channel and obstacle coming up!'

Breckon breathed heavily 'All the more reason to get him!'

'You'll get your chance, remember? Just have patience.'

'And in the meantime I've to suffer his mocking cocksureness and lose my dough!'

'Then either stop playing with him or beat him at his own game!'

'I can't stop playing! He'll think I'm frightened of him and to hell with that. No, I'll give him something to worry about.'

'What have you in mind?' The two men watched as Breckon stripped and put on dry clothes in the nook he had claimed as his own. He turned and laughed as he put on a thick flannel shirt.

'The answer's obvious, isn't it? The Grainger girl. They've been cosying up together for days. I might just try my luck in that direction. She must be easy or he wouldn't be sniffing around.'

The two men looked at him with respect and not a little scepticism.

'You sure do come up with some schemes, Charlie. I would never have thought that girl would lift her skirts!' Billy Revers spat over the rail. 'I wouldn't mind a bit of that skirt myself!'

'Any women'll lift her skirts if she's flattered enough. They're all the same under the skin, whether they're brought up in a parson's home or a brothel. Got the same urges under the ice-cold manner. I know, I've handled a few in my time!'

Billy laughed. 'I would never have believed it, Charlie. You don't strike me as a ladies' man.'

Charlie thrust his chin into Billy's face.

'Are you suggesting I don't know about women?' He was scowling and Billy stepped back a pace.

'Sorry, Charlie, I didn't mean you hadn't had experience, but I never thought you would be the one to be attracted to a real lady, that's all I meant.'

'Jesus H. Christ! You don't call that Grainger girl a real lady?'

'Well, her ma seems ladylike and they keeps theirselves to theirselves like, and the kids are well-mannered. Maybe a bit mischievous, but they don't spit and the boy don't piss over the rail.'

Charlie Breckon grunted. 'You wouldn't know a real lady if you saw one.'

'Maybe I wouldn't, but neither would you!' But Billy said it quietly as Charlie scrabbled around to find the half bottle of whiskey he had stashed away.

Charlie got a slap in the face from Amy Grainger the first time he made advances to her. He misread her polite interest when he doffed his cap and made a comment about the wonderful day and the scenery they were passing through as she would have done with any of the travellers with whom she came in contact.

Not that she mingled freely, for most of the time she kept to their cabin, but sometimes at night she would come out on deck to take the air, a relief from the stifling atmosphere.

Her suspicions were aroused, however, when he began regularly to come up on the top deck and his excuses for doing so were running low. So she was ready when one evening, partly drunk to give himself courage, he laid hands on her and her polite smile of greeting turned to disgust.

She struggled. He kissed her, inflamed by her resistance, and her doubled-up fist caught him on the jaw. He nearly went overboard once more.

'Sir, you forget yourself! You disgust me! Please go below or else I shall have to scream!' Her breasts heaved tantalisingly under the prim high-collared bodice. She rubbed at her mouth, contempt in every gesture.

He couldn't believe it!

No woman had ever rejected his advances and she had been quite friendly, acknowledging his overtures and smiling in that ladylike way. Suddenly he was angry. The bitch had been leading him on! She was doing it to make him keener! She was just like the others only she wasn't luring him with her cleavage. She looked so demure and inexperienced. He would bet his poke of gold dust that under that cool exterior there was a woman of passion.

He grabbed her about the waist.

'Come on, I know you're trying to make me keener. Well, I'm keen, believe me! Let's find some quiet corner and I'll show you what I've got for you!' He felt her stiffen and he squeezed her to him so that she could feel the bulge in his pants.

Then her knee came up in a savage thrust and shocked, and in agony, he collapsed.

She was staring down at his writhing figure when the hated sound of Saul Rhymer's voice came to him.

'This feller bothering you, Amy?' Breckon was lying on deck looking up at Saul Rhymer through pain-filled eyes.

'Not any more, Saul. Would you mind kicking him down the gangway to where he belongs?'

'It'll be a pleasure, Amy.' As Charlie Breckon scrambled up and was then kicked down the stairway, he vowed that the time would come when he would shoot the cocksure Rhymer in the guts and make that bitch pay before he killed her.

They became an obsession with him.

The *Star of the West* made her precarious way through channels kept open by much traffic going up and down the river. There was more activity now as they appoached Bismarck, the Cheyenne Agency and the Black Hills Landing and then on to Brule City, passing the forts with monotonous regularity.

The hazards now were wrecks of other boats and steamers caught up on sandbanks, often caused by trees swept down during winter storms and then covered with silt. Some of the wrecks were stripped bare as the cargoes had been

salvaged. They looked sad and lonely, rusting
away. Some were already half buried in the mud
of the river. She was a cruel taskmaster was the
Missouri River and the last home of many good
rivermen. Thousands had been lost over the years
and here and there were crosses to commemorate
the passing of a ship's crew or an outstanding
ship's master.

Passengers had come and gone as the steamer
docked and now, after leaving Sioux City, the crew
and passengers felt they were on the home run.
Soon they would dock at Omaha and take on more
stores. Then it would be the long run to Fort
Leavenworth, only stopping to refuel, and then
Kansas City, Lexington, Jefferson City, Wash-
ington, St Charles and then they would be in the
mouth of the Missouri and land at St Louis.

It all sounded so good as Captain Short
announced the itinerary and a ragged cheer went
up from the passengers. Tempers were getting
short; the guards Saul had organized were getting
fed up with the two-hour guard duty when nothing untoward happened. They grumbled. It was
all a waste of time.

'All right, all right.' Saul waved his arms at the
men grouped around him. 'It's better to be ready
and nothing happen than not be ready and get all
caught with our pants down. We've come this far,
surely we can see it to the bitter end?'

The Chiseller

'We're not getting paid!' someone shouted.

'You've got your life! Isn't that enough?'

But the grumbling went on and it was with reluctance some of the men volunteered to keep watch.

The river was now a busy thoroughfare between Sioux City and Omaha and Council Bluffs. Flat-bottomed boats and mackinaws and canoes sailed short-haul trips carrying supplies to the forts and to the outlying settlements. The rivermen were plentiful and if a man was willing to use his brawn to fight the river, a good living could be made. The business attracted all kinds of men who thought they could make a living on the backs of others.

It was after the steamer had left Council Bluffs and was steaming on to Nebraska City that the wreckers struck. The steamer was lying heavy in the water, for she had taken on board a new shipment of logs.

She was struggling wearily, her paddles making hard work of pushing the water aside and, at a bend in the river, they hit a new sandbank that the pilot and Captain Short had not reckoned to be there. There had also been a lot of thunder the night before and a lot of icy cold rain.

The current was stronger now and she ground herself tight on the sandbank. Captain Short cursed. It was going to be a long night and it looked as if the cargo would have to be shifted to lighten the load so that she might slide off the bank with the aid of the paddles and as much steam as could be raised.

The firemen sweated and built up steam. The first-class passengers went ashore and tents were rigged for the womenfolk and the children. The second-class passengers were pressed into helping to shift the vessel.

It was then that the wreckers struck. A grinning Charlie Breckon and his cronies laid about the pilot and Captain Short and left them unconscious in the wheelhouse.

The passengers on shore were paralysed with shock and the few guards who'd kept their guns tried in vain to stop the mad rush of the invaders. The military officers were the first to go down as they bunched together trying to defend the womenfolk.

There was much screaming and yelling amidst the explosion of arms as the wreckers swarmed aboard, ransacking the first-class cabins and searching out the hiding places of the miners who'd not been fortunate enough to go ashore and stash their gold.

It was soon over. The women and children were herded together ashore while the menfolk were held captive by a ring of armed grinning men.

The leader carried a small arsenal of pistols in

his belt and a sawn-off shotgun in his mighty fist strutted to and fro with Charlie Breckon following him like a lapdog.

Saul, who was standing well back, with Potman beside him, was furious with himself. He should have guessed the blackguard was up to something.

It had all happened so quickly he'd no time to get to Amy and her family who were already ashore. He and Potman were too busy heaving on ropes and helping to grasshopper the boat off the sandbank.

Now he watched the two men walk up and down assessing the passengers. Then the leader planted his feet apart and whacked his shotgun lightly against his leg.

'You men! I am going to make one announcement and one only! I am after gold and gold only. You may keep the rest except for what my men deem necessary for themselves. Every man here will step forward, in line, and bring his gold. That is his passport to freedom, starting now!'

'And if we don't?'

The man looked around the crowd of miners. 'Step out who said that!'

A burly miner with shoulders like an ox stepped forward. 'I've sweated blood for my stash, mister, and you're not getting it and to hell with yer!'

72

'Where is it?'

'Hidden and you'll not find it!'

The leader did not answer. He transferred the shotgun to his left hand and drew out a pistol from his belt and slowly lifted it and fired. The man's kneecap exploded like a scarlet rose.

He screamed and toppled over, thrashing at the ground in agony.

'Tell me where your gold is and I'll put you out of your misery,' he rasped.

'I'll see you in hell first!'

'Very well. You can go to hell the hard way!' He turned away from the groaning miner. 'Now everyone, if you're ready, please give me your offerings!' He gave a wide smile.

The men surrounding the prisoners cocked their weapons and took aim. The miners looked around and then shuffled into line and stepped forward. The crude bags of gold and gold dust, ranging from a few ounces to fifty or sixty pounds, were flung at the leader's feet.

Saul licked his lips as he drew near with Potman behind him. His stash was still on board hidden in his horse's manger, as were the horses, but he had his winnings in gold from the last few weeks. He hoped that would be enough to satisfy the bastard. He flung the small poke down defiantly. It went against the grain to do so, but those guns surrounding him gave him no choice.

He fumed inwardly and seeing Charlie Breckon's smug face fed the flames.

But Charlie Breckon scowled at the size of the poke.

'Come on, Rhymer, where's the rest? He's holding out, Roger. This is the bastard I was telling you of. He's the Chiseller, well known in the goldfields as the man who never misses a trick. A little bird told me he came aboard with the biggest ante ever seen in Fort Benton. Now where is it, Rhymer?'

Saul shook his head and lifted his hands.

'I'm sorry. Rumour has it wrong. That's all there is. I swear on my mother's grave!'

'You're a lying swine, Rhymer.' Breckon's gun came up and aimed for Rhymer's belly.

'Saul! Look out!' The little figure of Potman pushed Saul aside and took the bullet in his back. His eyes opened wide in disbelief before he collapsed.

Saul spun round and saw Potman go down and violent rage consumed him. He sprang for Breckon and grabbed him before he could take aim again, and dragged him behind Roger. 'Move and I'll blow you both to hell.' The two men stood frozen. 'Tell your men to drop their arms or I'll kneecap you both!' He jabbed Roger in the spine.

'All right, men, do as he says.'

'You fellers, collect the guns, pronto!'

It was then the first mighty crack of thunder came followed by more rain. It was a signal and, as Saul reacted to the sound, both men turned and lashed out at him. He went down in a sea of mud and then it seemed as if the whole world was fighting amidst the clamour of wind and rain and thunder, lit up with flashes of lightning.

Saul rolled and came up shooting. He caught Roger in the throat. Charlie Breckon was gone and, spitting mud, Saul clambered away to higher ground to look for Amy and her family.

He found her tending her mother with Robert and Sarah close by, shivering and cold with fear at what was going on around them.

Amy looked up at him, eyes wide and frightened.

'She's dying, Saul. I think she had a heart attack when those men attacked.'

He looked down at the peaceful figure wrapped up in a blanket. It was as if the old lady was sleeping, but there was no movement of her chest.

'I'm sorry, Amy.' He put an arm about her and Sarah crept closer and he held her too, while Robert came and stood tall and straight beside his mother and held her hand, struggling not to break down and cry.

The rain came down hard and pattered on the serene face and on all of them. What a sorry way to go, he thought compassionately. He rocked the girls gently in his arms.

'Don't be frightened, I'm looking after you now.'

There was a steady roar growing louder by the minute and then, as the men fought by the river's edge, a mighty flow of water rolled down the river, tumbling and thrashing into a white foam and greedily licking the sides and spreading over the bank taking all before it. The steamer stuck on the sandbank bucked and rocked, slid off the sandbar and careered sideways, only to lift herself on to the jagged teeth of rock, there to stay, battered and broken as the water rushed by.

Many men were swept away that night, both wreckers and passengers. The gold that was piled up into a heap was being washed downriver.

The water rose, bursting its banks and greedily drowning tree trunks and bushes. Small animals could be heard squeaking and fleeing into the night while huge trunks, roots torn from the ground, rolled and plunged downriver, battering the *Star of the West* as they swept by.

The steamer groaned and tugged, but was held fast by her weight and by one huge paddle ground on to the rocks below, her decks at an angle. All the while, the rain came down relentlessly.

It was nearly dawn when Saul was aware of horses crashing through the undergrowth. He was stiff, cold and wet and his teeth rattled. He was strangely weak for it had been a hard night and he'd collapsed a few hours earlier from fatigue.

He looked around. He and Amy and the children were on high ground. During the night he'd found a fur bale floating in the water and, dragging it to higher ground, had ripped it apart and made a rude shelter for them all, by tying it to low tree branches. The furs they used like blankets. Amy had stripped the children and herself and they'd clung together for warmth all through that dreadful night.

Saul had dug a grave for Mrs Grainger and laid her to rest with just a simple prayer over her. He grieved for Potman whose body had been swept away in the first rush of water. There was no sign or sounds of any survivors. All must have been swept away.

He had also scouted around and salvaged several packs that might yield clothes of one kind or another. Amy and the children needed dry clothes to survive the cold nights.

He sat up stiffly when he heard the horses in the distance and was in time to see Charlie Breckon and a small band of men, loaded up with whatever they could salvage, hightailing it south. He shook his fist after them. No doubt they would be heading for Nebraska City and the lure of liquor and easy women.

77

He swore an oath then to find Charlie Breckon and string him up, if it cost him the rest of his life.

Amy stirred and groaned and the children awakened at her movements and looked out bewilderedly at the surrounding devastated countryside. It was unbelievable how the country had changed. Gone was the lush greenery on each side of the meandering river, for now it looked like a lake and still the debris kept floating downstream. Bloated cattle and upturned canoes; the glistening black body of a buffalo swirled and pitched in the eddy of the current. Already the foul smell of decay gouged up from the silted bottom of the river was thickening. The water flowed brown and soupy and dead rats entangled in a woven mass of twigs and grasses added to the stench.

'Open those kitbags and see what we've got. If there's any kind of clothes at all, get 'em on.'

'What are you going to do? You're wet too. You should change.'

'Aye, I will do, but not until I've been on board and seen if there's anything to salvage. There might be food in the galley, and then there's the horses. They might be unharmed.'

'Saul, you'll be careful? The current's very strong!'

'I'm a good swimmer. I'll be fine.' He sounded more confident than he actually was.

'If you got swept away, I don't know what we'd do!' She held him close and Sarah started to cry.

He held both the girl and the child.

'Be brave, both of you. Robert, look after them and do everything your sister tells you.'

'Yes, sir.' Robert started opening one of the kitbags and Saul went off towards the swirling water without looking back.

Amy watched him go, heartsick and afraid. She, who had always prided herself on her courage, was now at her lowest ebb. First her mother gone and now Saul. Would he come back, or would he underestimate that roaring beast of a river and be swept away to be battered against the underlying rocks and then finally swallowed by a greedy river?

'Saul!' she called, but he did not look back. She turned away and then retched helplessly. Robert and Sarah came to hold her and mutter endearments and encouragement to her.

'He said he would come back, Amy, and Saul always keeps his promises,' Robert consoled, 'so don't cry. He'll come back, you see if he doesn't!'

They could only wait and watch and huddle together and it was the first time in his life that Robert wanted to pray.

'Oh, God, keep Saul safe and let him come back to us, and I'll never never tell another lie!'

FIVE

Saul made his way carefully along the swollen river until he was opposite the stricken steamer. There was a vast stretch of water separating them and it flowed with a menacing roar swirling and leaping above concealed rocks whipped up to a whitewater frenzy. It was the culmination of storms far into the Rocky Mountains, washing down from the many tributaries into the mighty Missouri.

The river could rise fast, but it could also go down fast because of the flow of water.

He eyed it with some trepidation. Would the old boat withstand the constant battering, or would it break up before the waters receded? But, what was more important, could he survive the current and clamber aboard?

He took several deep breaths. He had to try. He couldn't sit on his haunches and watch the mad water race. He had to do something. If those horses were still alive, they could be the salvation of them all.

He moved back upstream and gauged how the current would sweep him along once he was in the water. He saw the ripples passing over an outcrop of rock and knew if he could reach it, he would be out of the millrace for enough time to gather his strength.

He stripped to his long johns and then for a few minutes flexed his muscles and took several deep breaths, all the while watching the ever-racing water.

Then, closing his eyes and taking a mighty breath, he plunged in facing upstream. At once the cold hit him and he was battling with the current, but it had its effect and he slewed out into midstream, gaining a little and being swept nearer the outcrop. He fought the water and after what seemed an age he grabbed for the rock itself, but it was smooth and greasy and for long anxious moments he thought he would be swept away far past the grounded boat.

Then he found a crevice in the rock and his fingers clung with desperate strength and he was hanging on although buffeted by the strength of the current. His knees and hips were grazed and bruised, but he gritted his teeth and prayed for strength and determination to swim that last hundred yards.

He could just make it, before the river swept him away downstream, if he could but battle the piercing cold.

Then above the roar of the water, he heard a scream and looked back to the riverbank and saw Amy, dressed in a man's pants, shirt and heavy lumber jacket, wildly waving an arm and holding up a coiled rope.

He took a chance and waved back, again grabbing the rock with both hands, and watched as she tried to throw the rope to him.

'Throw it out further upstream so that it drifts towards the rock,' he bawled, but his words were lost in the wind and roar of the water.

Three times she tried and hauled in the rope but the third time she must have figured on how the current was running for on the fourth try he watched the rope floating down towards him and he made a grab for it as it was streaking by.

He felt the pull of the rope and thanked God she was practical enough to wrap the rope around the stump of a tree.

He had a fleeting vision of her, wet hair streaming behind her, the bulky jacket giving the illusion size and strength she didn't have. He managed to grip the rock with his knees and ankles as he whipped the end of the rope about his waist and tied a clumsy knot.

It gave him confidence and added strength for

the ordeal to come. Then, unable to cling any longer to the overhanging rock he plunged in again, allowing the current to sweep him into the millrace and so thrashing his way towards the stricken boat.

He just made it. For one wild moment he thought he'd missed it. He struggled like a madman and caught hold of one of the sunken paddles as the boat lay obscenely on her side like a spiked goose with her flat bottom up and one set of paddles in midair.

He thanked God that the other huge set of paddles was underwater and he could get a toehold and fight the force that threatened to sweep him away. He climbed upwards until he found himself out of the water and tumbled on to the sloping deck.

He lay winded and gasping, deafened, water streaming from him for it seemed like aeons of time but it must have been only a few minutes. When he rose to his feet, his leg muscles were like jelly. He clung on to the grotesquely drunken rail and moved forward cautiously.

His priority was to find food in the galley and see if the horses in their makeshift stalls were still alive.

The frightened nickering raised his hopes. It would be too good to be true if they were unhurt. The deck was tilted at an angle and he had to remove a lot of loose debris before he could reach them. But the horses were standing on their legs, all askew, with their halters keeping them from rolling on top of each other. Only one of Potman's pack animals had come to grief. It had slipped and fallen and the animal next to it had leant heavily against it, suffocating the poor beast.

The horses flung their heads and whinnied in greeting and now Saul had to devise a way of getting them off the boat. But first he must find out if there was any food not ruined by the water.

It took quite a while to negotiate the galley and all the while the old boat rocked and strained at the bombardment of water.

He found a sack of flour that had missed the water, a bag of coffee beans, some tins of peaches and a side of bacon still swinging from the rafters. There was bread, but it was sodden, and several joints of meat polluted by the river water. Then he found a bag of chilli beans and his hopes rose. They could get by for several days if they were careful and he could hunt fresh meat.

The best find was the cache of bullets. He filled a sugarbag and wrapped it in some oiled silk he found in Captain Short's quarters that had protected the boat's log.

Then he made his way to his own horse and to the manger and to his relief he found his saddle-bags where he had left them.

He was too tired to cheer, but went to the task
of calming the horses with a greater will. He
saddled two horses, stowing the saddle-bags and
rolling up the bag of bullets into his sleeping bag
and making all shipshape. Then, leading each
horse slowly and carefully along the raised up
deck, he took the rope tied around his waist and
fastened it to the first horse's bridle. Moving to
the stern he looked about him and found an axe
and hacked away at the painted white rails until
he'd made a wide enough opening. He led the
trembling animal forward, gave a mighty shout
and a sharp slap on the rump and the horse
plunged into the fast current and started to swim.

Amy, on the bank, saw what was happening
and hauled on the rope. Gradually the swimming
animal trod water and heaved itself ashore, where
Amy tethered it and threw the rope back to Saul.

Potman's horse proved harder to handle
because he wasn't used to being loaded up, but the
remaining pack animal took to the water like a
duck.

It took the best part of four hours before Saul
was lying exhausted on the riverbank, with Amy
kneeling beside him, holding his head and tipping
whiskey into his mouth. Her face was pale and
drawn.

'Saul, answer me. Don't die on me now!'

He choked on the whiskey and opened his eyes.

'I'm not ready yet to hand in my chips! Just let me get my breath back.'

'I've been so frightened. I never thought you'd make it.'

For a long moment he didn't answer and when it came he sounded exhausted.

'I wouldn't have if you hadn't brought that rope.' He groped for her hand and sighed. 'I'm proud of you, girl.' Then he closed his eyes again.

She shook him.

'Damn you, Saul! This is no time to lie sleeping! You'll die of pneumonia. You must get out of those wet clothes!'

He shook his head, eyes closed.

'Leave me alone, I want to sleep!'

She looked about her. What would shock him awake? She saw the three horses tethered together and remembered Saul's gun she'd brought with the rope. She'd slipped it into Saul's saddle-bag for safety.

She found it and came back and stood before the inert body lying like one dead. She bit her lip and cocked the gun. She'd never fired one in her life. Then, taking aim a couple of feet from him, she pulled the trigger and the bullet slammed into the ground sending up a shower of sticky mud. The blast knocked her over and she trembled with shock.

Saul, at the sound of the blast, was up on his

knees looking around like a mountain cat at bay. His eyes found Amy stretched out and a groan escaped his lips.

'Amy! My God! I'll kill the bastard who did this!' He cradled her to him, only to find that he wasn't holding a dead body but a very much alive girl who was shaking both with laughter and relief.

She clung to him. 'I had to do it. It was the only way to shock you awake.'

'You mean you shot *at* me?'

'Well, just a little bit. You must keep moving. We've got to get back to the children, they'll be wondering where we are.'

'Didn't you tell them?'

'No, they were asleep and I hadn't the heart to awaken them. It seemed best to leave them undisturbed.'

'Come on then. They'll be out of their minds with worry.'

They found them hungry, bewildered and frightened. Sarah cried when she saw them come back to their temporary camp, but both children were more cheerful after their first good meal for two days.

The rain had ceased during the night and Saul watched the river carefully. It was no longer rising. Perhaps soon it would shrink back to its customary level. The going would be tough, for the ground would be a morass for a while and they dared not travel too far inland to find dry ground.

'Where shall we head for?' Amy asked.

'We go downstream and head for Nebraska City. There are wagon trails crossing the country. With luck we might hit one of them.'

'And what about Breckon and his men?'

Saul gazed long and thoughtfully into the distance. 'If I was him I'd make for the city and disperse the gang, take my cut and get to hell out of it.'

'Do you think we might run into him?'

'There's a chance, I suppose, but I doubt it. We're a couple of days behind him. I think we'll be safe enough.'

The packhorse took their pitifully small amount of gear and Saul and Amy rode the two horses with Sarah in front of Saul and Robert in front of Amy. Saul took charge of the precious saddle-bags, the ammunition and the guns.

They followed the river from a distance and, when it bent sharply in a loop, Saul climbed the nearest bluff to follow its trail. They took chances and cut across country and joined the river again further downstream. It saved hours of futile travel.

One night as they crouched by their small fire and the children were asleep, rolled up in the furs they'd brought with them, Amy asked softly, 'We'll make it, won't we?'

His arm about her, he hugged her to him.

'Of course we will.' But he wasn't sure. He was no trapper with a trapper's knowledge of how to survive in the wilds. He'd spent his life at the gambling tables, conning city slickers. He sighed. Already he'd found it wasn't easy hunting fresh meat. He hadn't quite got the knack of coming up on the windward side of his prey. They upped their heads and sniffed and bounded away before he could aim and fire.

His bag up to date had been poor. A couple of jack-rabbits and a very young deer who'd lost its mother.

'We're getting short of flour and coffee,' she said tentatively.

'Goddammit! I know!' Fear made him irritable. 'Do you think I don't realize what we're up against? I don't even know how many goddamn miles we are from civilization!'

'What about the woodyards? We could find help at one of them.'

'What, after this flood? I doubt there'll be any still operating. We can't count on any help from along the river.'

Suddenly Amy started to cry and her weeping struck him through the heart. He held her close and rocked her like a baby.

'I've told you, Amy, we'll get to Nebraska City and, by God, we will!'

The Chiseller

They had been travelling for nearly a week when they hit the wagon trail. There was the smell of cows and it didn't take an Indian scout to deduce that a herd had passed that way very recently. Cowpats were everywhere, mosquitoes buzzed and the stench wrinkled their noses.

It was the best aroma in the world!

The horses carrying double were tiring. They walked with heads down, no spring in their step, but now Saul whipped up his mount and the others followed.

Suddenly he was more hopeful than he had been for days. Amy was no longer drooping and, when Saul dismounted with Robert to ease his horse's load, she and Sarah followed suit.

Soon, the children were laughing and running ahead, keen and eager to be the first to locate the passing herd.

Then, as they came to the brow of the next hill, they saw the cloud of dust ahead down in the valley that ran alongside the river which cut it in half.

'Look!' Robert cried, dancing up and down with excitement, 'There it is! I can see the chuck wagon rolling along behind!' Saul and Amy, with Sarah alongside, stood and watched the dimly seen herd of cows moving on towards Nebraska City.

It took them until dusk to come upon them and it was only because the trail boss had the herd settled early for the night that they managed to join up with them.

The horses needed rest and food.

The trail boss stared at the sorry-looking party that had materialized out of the gathering dusk.

'Well now, what have we here?'

Saul, leading his horse with Robert clinging to the saddle, Amy and Sarah crowding close, the packhorse trailing behind, came to a halt before him.

'You the boss of this outfit?'

'I sure am. I'm Jed Crawford and I run the JC brand. What in hell are you doing with a woman and kids out here?'

'I'm Saul Rhymer. We were on board the *Star of the West* when the storm struck and she went aground. Then we were hijacked by wreckers looking for gold.'

'And did they find any?'

'I guess so. They rode away. I managed to salvage the horses from the wreck.'

'You went into that water in full spate?

Saul nodded.

'Gee, mister, you had balls to do that! Come on, now, Cookie will find you something to eat and you can tell me all about it.' He looked at Amy and the children's bedraggled appearance. 'You sure look all in, ma'am, and the kids too. A nice plate of stew'll put you right.'

The Chiseller

The cowpunchers not engaged in putting the cows to bed, gathered round and listened to Saul's tale of betrayal and the subsequent mayhem.

They listened avidly, the lowing of cattle in the background and the faint sound of cowpunchers humming as they made their rounds and settled the cows for sleeping.

At last Saul was done. Amy and the children had long since gone to sleep, from the heat of the camp-fire and their full bellies.

'So you're not the girl's husband?'

Saul shook his head.

'She was aboard with her mother and her brother and sister,' he said, at Jed Crawford's enquiring look.

'Is she any good at patching a feller up? We've got a cowpoke with a busted leg. He got caught up in a stampede further back and he's travelling in the chuck wagon with Cookie.'

'Yeah, she's got a cool head and skilful fingers.'

'He needs his leg kept clean for fear of gangrene. Could she look after him?'

'I don't see why not.'

'Good. Then you can take Ned's place. We're short of a man on the job. We're running a thousand head for the Nebraska market and that takes in the fort too. We want a man to hunt mavericks. Could you do that?'

Saul was on the point of saying he'd never been

93

on a cattle drive, then shut his mouth and nodded.

'Then you're on the payroll. The kids can help Cookie gather firewood and such. He'll keep 'em amused too. He's a rare one for his tall tales is Esau.'

And so it was that Amy found herself nursing an absolute stranger and also patching up small cuts and bruises from the other cowpunchers who seemed to walk into trouble far too often, until Jed Crawford told them forcefully and in no uncertain terms to leave the girl alone and get on with the job.

Saul found it a gut-churning job to seek out and chivvy the half-wild mavericks back into the herd. They lowered their wide horned heads and charged him on occasion, the older steers being the most ornery.

He rescued them out of rock crevices, out of swamps with his lariat, and watched the other cowpunchers for tips to make the job easier.

He made friends with one short little fellow, bowlegged, dried up like a prune, who always smelled of strong tobacco and sweaty horses and who usually had a corncob pipe clenched between teeth which were stained tobacco-brown. Wall-eyed Pete was no painting, but he was honest and he didn't grumble at conditions or take sly lustful looks at Amy. He was too old for all that.

'You keep close by me and you'll soon learn,' he

said, one night after Amy had bandaged up Saul's thigh. 'You watch their eyes and when their heads go down that's when you look for trouble and be ready to jump like a grasshopper.'

They worked well together and took the grave-yard spell from midnight to dawn, when they would circle the cows, humming a monotonous tune to lull the beasts lying close together. Sometimes a steer would lift its head and give a bellow and then a ripple of movement would run through the herd, even a few staggering to their feet, disturbed and confused.

Then it was that the singing was imperative for if the leaders of the herd were startled, then God knew how far they would run. No trail boss wanted a stampede on his hands. It wore the beasts out and turned them into four-legged bags of bones, instead of prime beef in the stockyards.

Saul saw little of Amy at this time, or the children, and time dragged. He told Pete about Charlie Breckon and his vow to get him. Pete sucked on his empty pipe.

'I knew Charlie Breckon years ago. He was always a cocky swine as a young 'un. Started a lot of unrest amongst the Sioux. He's a bad man to cross. Seems like he hasn't changed. He hangs out with a crowd at a place near St Charles, or he did do, last time I heard about him.'

Pete eyed Saul speculatively.

The Chiseller

'Lots of people would like him dead. Thinks he's a card slicker. Used to play with the big-timers in Nebraska City. Maybe still does. You might find him at the Longhorn Saloon, the cattlemen's haunt.'

Saul looked at him. 'That a fact?'

The old man nodded. 'A leopard don't change his spots. If he's got gold, he'll be back at the tables, I could bet on it!'

Saul nodded. 'I think I'll turn in; it'll soon be the graveyard shift.' He didn't sleep, however. His mind was on Breckon and the problem of what to do with Amy and the children while he went looking for vengeance.

He was still thinking about it when he roused Pete from sleep with a mug of coffee from the pot standing in the banked-up embers of the campfire.

'Wakey, wakey, Pete, old son. Time we were up nursing those ornery critturs!'

Pete awakened with a groan.

'Why did you have to do that? I was in the middle of something interesting with a tart with big tits!'

'Chance would be a good thing. Now shake those old bones and let's get riding. We've got to do something to earn our keep!'

Later, when they returned saddlesore and weary to the chuck wagon, it was to find several of the cowpunchers lined up with tin mugs and plates ready for the rough but substantial breakfast that was the main meal of the day. It had to be good.

Amy was helping Cookie. She looked pretty and feminine, now wearing her own clean clothes. Saul noticed that all the men doffed their hats to her and no colourful language was being used. He joined the queue and was rewarded with a smile along with the coffee and steaming stew with a good hunk of fresh panbread on top. It smelled good.

He was lounging close by after he'd eaten, when he saw Luke Marriot shuffle over to her for a second time. Cookie had his back turned, intent on clearing up before his wagon rolled with the herd.

He saw Amy flinch as Luke Marriot crowded her some. The man's back was to Saul and he didn't see what happened. Then Amy took a step backwards and she looked furious. Saul was on his feet in a flash.

'This man bothering you, Amy?'

Luke Marriot, grinning, turned to Saul. 'No need to get all-fired up, mister. Just complimenting the lady on her baking. Cookie's bread ain't a patch on hers!'

'Is that so? Is that the right of it, Amy?'

Amy looked uncomfortable.

The Chiseller

'Are you calling me a liar, mister?'

'Yes. What are you going to do about it?'

'This is what!' Luke Marriot lunged forward, and aimed his fist at Saul's chin.

Saul saw it coming and dodged and came up with a haymaker of his own, rocking the other man on his heels. Crouching and turning to face Marriot as the man ducked and dived around him, he said tauntingly, 'Come on, let's see what you're made of. Let's see if you've as much sass with me as you have with a young girl!'

Then they were plunging and rolling, biting and kicking, over and over on the ground, locked together in a mass of arms and legs.

Cookie turned with an oath and dragged Amy clear of the thrashing legs. She was stunned with shock. Robert and Sarah watched the ruckus from behind the chuck wagon, wide-eyed and frightened.

The men gathered round, shouting encouragement to Luke, still a little suspicious of the newcomer. Jed Crawford dismounted from his horse, furious that the men weren't ready to move out.

'What the hell's going on here?' he roared. 'We've got to get these cows moving!'

He made to wade in and separate the combatants but his foreman spoke up for all the men.

'Gee, boss, at this rate it won't last long.' He

watched the furious onslaught and assessed the rate of blood spilled. 'Give the boys a break. We don't often see a damned good fight, and this one sure is. I bet you even money, the young feller knocks out Luke!'

Jed Crawford grinned. 'All right, you've persuaded me. I'll put my money on Luke. He's a wily bastard, used to dirty fighting. I'll lay you five dollars!'

'Done, boss!' They slapped their hands together.

Jed Crawford drew on a cigar as he watched. His money was on Luke, but he could see promise in the strong shoulders of the newcomer. The feller was worth studying. He might be inexperienced nursing cows, but he could sure move his body.

The fight finished abruptly and in spectacular fashion. There were two hard swipes to the face and while Luke Marriot staggered back, shaking his head, Saul caught him by the scruff of the neck and the seat of his pants, and lifted him with muscle-cracking ease above his head and bent him backwards like a bow.

Then he swung him round and round while Luke yelled.

'Do you apologize to the lady?' Saul bawled, at the top of his voice.

'Yes . . . yes! For God's sake put me down. You're breaking my back!'

Then Saul heaved and Luke hit the ground with such force the watching men heard bones crack. Saul was on him like a mountain lion, dragging him to his knees.

'Now apologize, damn you!'

Luke groaned. 'I apologize.'

'And you'll keep away from her in future?'

'Yes . . . yes! I'll not even think about her!'

Saul gave him a push and he sprawled into the dust. Saul looked around at the other men.

'And that goes for you all. Miss Amy is a lady. Remember it.'

The men moved away and forked their horses. They would talk about the fight later, but now the important thing was getting the herd rolling. Jed Crawford paid up cheerfully, a small price to pay to watch a good fight.

However, he was a worried man. He wished he'd never come across the small group. Womenfolk were hell on a cattledrive and if they didn't reach Nebraska City soon, there might be other incidents concerning the woman.

Men were like animals when they hadn't seen a woman for months on end. God knows, he'd seen some of the quietest men go loco for the want of a woman.

It was more than a week later when catastrophe struck.

The air had grown hot and humid. Clouds

were gathering and, in the distance, thunder could be heard rolling round the hills. Flashes of lightning lit up the sky and made the bedded down herd restless.

Jed Crawford doubled up the nightwatch ready for trouble. Saul and Pete had done their stint and, after their evening meal, rolled themselves in their blankets to be ready later if they were needed.

Saul had spent some brief time with Amy and the children and was satisfied that there had been no more overtures either by Luke Marriot or any of the others. Indeed, all the men were wary in her presence.

He'd chosen to sleep in a small stand of trees not far from the chuck wagon which stood well back and at the side of the herd. The wagon always travelled at the side, so that they didn't ride into the duststorm created by the steers as they ambled along, munching the dried grass as they went.

Amy and the children slept in a lean-to shelter, a tarpaulin that Cookie had rigged up and fastened roughly to the side of the wagon. It gave them a little privacy and was welcomed by Amy.

It was an inborn instinct that awakened Saul. One moment he was sleeping the sleep of the exhausted and the next he was wide awake, eyes open and straining for some sound. He lay listening hard. Had he heard an animal padding around the camp?

He threw back his blanket and sat up. In the near distance he could hear and smell the restless cows and in the far distance the comforting sound of men humming. So all was well with the herd.

Then he heard the strange whimpering sound again which must have awakened him. Getting up quietly he grabbed his rifle and moved out into the open.

Then he saw them, two dark figures, one dragging the other, moving away from the lean-to tent. The whimpering sounds were coming from Amy and she had Luke Marriot's arm about her shoulders and his dirty hand clamped across her face. In the other hand, Saul saw the glint of steel in the moonlight.

'Let her go, Marriot,' he called softly, 'or I'll kill you where you stand!'

'And risk a stampede!' The other man laughed, a high-pitched sound as if he'd flipped. 'Make a move, mister, and I'll stick this knife into her. She be plaguing me long enough. Now I'm going to teach her what a real man can do!'

'A real man? You can't even fight!' Saul taunted.

'Goddamn you, Rhymer! I know your game. You're trying to make me madder'n a bear who's lost her cubs. I don't play, buster, so you either let me pass or I stick the girl. Right?'

'You'll not get away with it, Marriot.'

'What makes you think I won't?'

'Because there's someone right behind you, mister, and his gun is covering your backbone!'

Saul suddenly experienced the familiar exhilaration that occurred during his many bluffs, when success hung on a pinnacle.

Luke Marriot jumped and looked around, the knife slipping from Amy's throat, and in that instant, Saul sent up a prayer that Amy wouldn't move. He shot Luke Marriot in the side of the head above his left ear.

For a moment, Luke Marriot stood upright and then slowly slid to the ground pulling Amy with him. Saul tossed his gun aside and dragged a sobbing Amy free. He held her close, sweat dripping from him.

'You're all right?'

She clung to him and nodded. He kissed her. Then he became aware of another more menacing sound which rolled on and on. It was mixed up with frantic cows lowing and throwing back their heads. Those that were still lying down heaved themselves to their feet and joined in the stampede. There was nothing the boys on the edge of the herd could do but watch helplessly as the leaders started their mindless running.

'Goddammit! Who was that shooting?' bawled Jed Crawford. But no one answered for Saul was forking his horse and, along with bowlegged Pete, was galloping into the night to help control the running beasts. In the distance, the thunder grew louder and the lightning came at shorter intervals.

It was going to be one long hell of a night.

SIX

For what seemed hours, Saul raced along behind Pete, keeping pace with the frenzied cows. They were a running mass which a man could have sprinted across from side to side, but, as they ran, they left small bodies behind, those of calves unable to keep up and trampled into the ground, There was no time for inspection now; the cost would be counted later.

Then the lightning cut across the sky, showing the moving bodies in an eerie greenish glow.

Saul could hear distant shots as the punchers strove to guide the leaders ahead into an inner curve, eddying the beasts into a running circle. It was a dangerous business, for the cowpunchers who rode experienced cow horses had to brave the solid banks of running flesh, keep up or be submerged by the force of the animals galloping behind, and to know when to fire their guns into the air and divert those hoary old leaders and put the brakes on the panting, now tiring, beasts.

There was the right time and the wrong time to do this. Many a good puncher had got it wrong and paid the price, leaving only a mangled body, hardly enough to bury.

But, if instinct and experience proved right, then a herd could be saved from itself. Jed Crawford was an experienced operator, but it took until well past dawn to turn the beasts in on themselves, and stem the tide.

When the sun was well up, it revealed a sorry sight. Cows standing and lying exhausted, others wandering slowly in a confused state, lowing softly for calves that were now lost forever; those in milk, bellowing in pain of overfull udders.

Saul and Pete walked their horses around the perimeter of the spread-out mass of animals, noting stragglers and estimating damage. Two cows had been shot, crippled from broken legs and then trampled. The flesh was no good to eat because it was cut to ribbons and pounded to pulp.

Pete looked at Saul sideways.

'Jed isn't going to like this. Are you going to tell him how it started?'

Saul fingered his whiskered chin. 'What d'you think? He'll want to know about Marriot. There's the bullet wound.'

Pete grunted. 'If I were you I'd keep quiet and

tell that gal of yours to keep her mouth shut. The boss has more on his plate than to worry about a dead cowpuncher. This lot will have cost him dear. He'll be in a rare temper for the next few days!'

It was decided to rest the cows for the next twenty-four hours and it was nearly at the end of that time when Marriot was found, that is what was left of him.

For the scavengers had been out and it wasn't only dead calves they'd gnawed at. Marriot was not a pretty sight. The boys who'd known and worked with Marriot over a long time, buried him quick, glad to get it over. The general opinion was that the poor bastard had got his when the cows began the stampede.

Pete and Saul stood silently by, hats in hand, and never said a word. Amy watched with a sense of guilt from the safety of the chuck wagon and prayed for the man's soul.

But they put all that behind them when finally they hit Nebraska City and the stockyards and Saul and Amy shook hands with Jed Crawford and the boys and thanked them for their help. Saul had a private word with wall-eyed Pete.

'If you want a change, old-timer, you can kick in with us. I'm sure Amy would like to have you around.'

Pete grinned. 'Now that's mighty fine of you, Saul, and I appreciate it, but I've punched cows all my life and I ain't gonna change now. Give Miss Amy my respects and the kids too. I'll miss you all like hell, but it wouldn't work. I could never settle in one place. I've been a mover all my life. I'll die on the move. Right?'

Saul nodded. He knew the urge to look over the next hill. It was part of something that was untamed in a man.

'Well, if you ever want to come and visit, you can ask around in St Louis. Me and Amy aim to settle somewhere near her folks, God willing. We've got a sight of travel yet from here to St Louis and I've got some business to attend to first.'

Pete looked sly.

'It's Charlie Breckon, isn't it? He's got right into your craw.'

'Yep. I'll see the whites of his eyes yet!'

'What are you aiming to do?'

'I'm gonna settle Amy and the kids in the best hotel in town and then I'm going after the bastard. Someone will know where he is. A man like him doesn't just disappear into a crowd.'

'Then if you're set on it, God help you! He plays dirty and you'll have to watch your back!'

Saul smiled. 'I've got his measure. His weakness is poker. I'll get him!'

'But he'll recognize you! He'd never sit in with you!'

'Oh, yes, he will. He'll come running when he hears there's a gambler in town who's throwing gold around.'

Pete stared at him and licked his lips.

'You carrying gold? Well, I'm damned! Now there's a thing Charlie Breckon likes more than poker and that's gold. But how will you manage to get to him face to face?'

Saul put a finger to his nose.

'Now that would be telling! What you don't know, can't hurt you.'

Pete scowled. 'I'd never split on you! I'm your pard!'

'Sorry, Pete.' He put an arm about the bent old shoulders. 'Nothing personal, but if Charlie did get wind of you being my pard, you might be in danger. Look on it that I'm protecting us both. Right?'

Pete nodded reluctantly.

'You're playing a dangerous game, Saul. He's got a stack of men behind him.'

'I've taken on better men than him in the Montana goldfields and I'm still in one piece. Don't worry, Pete, it doesn't matter how you treat a cat, it lands on its feet!'

Later, he convinced Amy that she and the children should go out and explore Nebraska City and maybe buy some new clothes, enjoy the sights and recover from their ordeal while he went about his business, and that she was not to worry if his business lasted a few days. He was vague about her question of how long.

'Long enough to finish it,' he answered gruffly and wouldn't expound any further, no matter how many questions she asked. She was both disturbed and sulky when he left her.

Sarah definitely upset him when she looked up at him with trusting eyes and asked, 'You're not leaving us for good? We need you, Saul.'

He bent and hugged her close and kissed her on the forehead.

'I'll be back. While I'm gone Robert will look after you both, won't you, Robert?'

Robert straightened his back and stretched himself as tall as he could.

'Yes, sir! I'll look after them.'

Now, Saul smiled at the memory as he looked into the long cheval mirror at his new self. Robert was a great kid and if he wanted to be a doctor, as his father and grandfather had been, then he'd make damn sure the kid got his chance.

The salesman behind him picked fluff from the shoulders of the long, black, snug-fitting jacket.

'A perfect fit, I must say, sir. It looks as if it was made for you. If you pardon me for saying so, I have never seen a better figure for showing off the coat, the trousers and the vest . . . dare I say that you have the taste of a gentleman?'

'You don't mean that of a gambler?' Saul laughed at the embarrassment on the man's face. He eyed the black and gold embroidered vest doubtfully. 'Maybe I should try the brocade. . . .'

'Oh, no, sir! This is more distinguished and more the style worn in St Louis and New Orleans. It came in our latest shipment from St Louis.'

'Then I'll take your advice. Now, I want a plain grey vest for everyday use and one cut a little looser under the arms to accommodate a holster. Have you such a thing?'

While the salesman hurried away to look over his stock, Saul eyed himself once again in the mirror. There was no resemblance to the man on the riverboat. His curly black hair was trimmed close to the head, his beard was shaved off, and only a luxuriant moustache curled upwards, meeting the sideburns that gave him a rakish air.

The long frock coat, white, frilled shirt and cravat with a stickpin, gave him elegance. His shiny boots overlapping the tight breeches, gave him the air of a fop, a man of the tables, a night bird of the city.

He would wager his last gold nugget that Charlie Breckon would never recognize him, especially in the yellow light of the oil lamps of the professional cardrooms.

He was satisfied. Even Amy wouldn't recognize him now!

He changed into the dove-grey vest and then
adjusted the frock coat and looked at himself at
all angles. Yes, he would do. He would pass as a
wealthy member of a well-established city family.

He paid in dollar bills, leaving his old clothes in
a bundle with instructions that they should be
burned. He also tipped the salesman five dollars,
knowing that his instructions would be met.

Now for the next port of call. His destination
was the biggest bank in Nebraska City where the
best gold assayer had his chambers. The
Nebraska Corporate Bank had impressive
premises built of granite. The gold and the accu-
mulated stash of dollar bills were now in a leather
valise, the worn saddle-bags, his saddle and horse
were in the finest livery in town.

He jammed his new, deep-brimmed, Spanish
caballero hat more firmly on his head at a rakish
angle, and walked up the steps of the imposing
frontage with back straight and the air of a man
who ordered things done.

The teller saw at a glance that the customer
was a man who could make trouble and at once
went to seek the manager who came, rubbing his
hands, smiling the unctuous smile of a man who
could smell money and power.

'Good afternoon. What can we do for you, sir?'

'I wish to rent a safety deposit box for a few
days.'

The Chiseller

The smile disappeared. 'Does sir have an account with us? I do not recall seeing you before.'

'No. I'm a traveller on my way to St Louis, and staying in Nebraska City with friends for a few days. I would appreciate the convenience in the usual way.' Saul coughed into his hand.

The manager's eyes brightened.

'You wouldn't be newly arrived from the Montana goldfields? Many gentlemen stop off here for relaxation and entertainment before moving on to other parts. We're famed for our hospitality, especially to the gold speculators.' Now it was the manager's turn to cough into his hand.

Saul smiled. 'Then we are in agreement? I will show my appreciation in the usual way whatever the rental.'

'One moment, please, while I get you a key. I just recall there is one empty box. I will show you the strong-room myself.'

The steel-lined room was lined with numbered boxes of three sizes, small, medium and large.

The manager looked at the bulky valise.

'I think you will need our largest box.' He smiled ingratiatingly and the smile broadened when Saul handed over a wad of bills.

'An act of good faith. I shall pay the rental when I come to collect, and now ... please?' The manager took the hint and left the room, quietly closing the door behind him.

It didn't take long to open the valise and count out the roll of bills he estimated he would need. Then he sorted through the remaining gold nuggets that he'd kept when turning the smaller stuff, plus the dust, into dollars at the assay office; the Missouri Gold Smelters Corporation bought gold, no questions asked. Now, all he had left to take with him as a lure for Charlie Breckon were the varying sized pieces of raw gold. He knew basically how much every nugget was worth.

He was satisfied and he packed away into the valise the impressive sight of nuggets in a leather pouch and a wad of large denomination dollar bills he would use during his poker games. The rest was locked away in the safety deposit box.

The next item on the agenda was to find Charlie Breckon's hunting ground and he reckoned it wouldn't be hard to do. The man was an addict and he would no more be able to resist the green baize than an alcoholic his booze.

He visited a few bars and saloons, drank beer watched and asked questions. The menfolk were wary of a stranger in their midst, especially one who asked questions but didn't answer them.

The womenfolk were easier to handle. They came at him like butterflies, gaudy and perfumed. They were all colours, from young, satin-skinned quadroons to white fat or thin, leather-cheeked women with greedy eyes, to newly freed blacks

114

who were now supporting their menfolk in the only way they knew.

They would all talk, for a price, and most of them wanted to do more than talk. They smelled success in his fresh turned-out appearance.

'Charlie Breckon? Why be interested in him? Why not come upstairs first and I'll give you a real Nebraska City welcome? Then we can talk afterwards,' one delightful, nearly young woman with a shapely figure, asked him. In the old days he would have grinned cheerfully and gone upstairs. He smelled her fresh perfume and was aware of his arousal. But he remembered Amy and somehow the excitement was gone from the encounter. His heart wasn't in it.

She scowled and turned a smooth, creamy shoulder from him. 'If you won't, you won't,' she said petulantly, 'but it's very queer. I've forgotten all about Charlie Breckon. Who's he?' She left him and went smiling towards a newcomer and held out her hand.

'Darling! Where've you been this last week? I've missed you. How about buying me a drink?'

Saul smiled and shrugged.

He had better luck in the Golden Nugget Saloon. He saw several gamblers sitting at a table in the far end of the long bar.

'I see the boys are playing early.' He nodded to the barman as he paid for his beer.

'Yeah, they're out-of-towners. Come in every month. They start early and play all day and all night until there's only one left sitting up. I've seen the kitty sky high and the winner too glassy eyed to know anything about it. Mind you, there's a minder, and God help anyone who might think to grab the take! He shot a man's hand off once and there was a helluva to-do about it.'

'I bet you can recall some risky situations.' Saul, lounging on the bar, grinned.

'Yeah, I could write a book, if I could write. I been barman here since this place was a soddy in the middle of nowhere. I could tell you some tales.'

'You know Charlie Breckon?'

'Oh, aye, who doesn't? Plays in the backroom for gold when he's in town, which ain't too often. He's known as Mr Gold-dust himself. Quite a guy, but a mean bastard. Never tips and treats the girls something rotten.'

'Like that, is he? Where does he hang out?'

The barman looked at Saul quizzically.

'You not aiming to take him? He's got guys watching his back and if you think you can play his kind of poker, you must think you're goddamned good!'

'Where did you say he hangs out?'

'I didn't. But if you want to know, ask at the Red Garter brothel on the end of Main Street. He's got a woman there who doesn't seem to mind him beating her up. He pays her well to do so.' The barman returned to polishing glasses.

'Thanks. I might just look her up. What's her name?'

'Fullalove. Nell Fullalove, but don't tell her I told you.'

Saul grinned and tossed him a dollar.

'Thanks, pal. If you don't talk, I don't talk.'

The barman laughed and tossed the coin into the air, then pocketed it.

'Good hunting, mister, and good luck. You'll need it!'

Saul left the bar and walked past a drugstore, then stopped to read an advertisement for an apothecary cream. It amused him for it appeared to have magic properties. 'It is made from the same formula as did the Incas make it in ancient times for those unfortunates who would suffer the pox, toxic swellings, concretion of the bowels, along with the killing of nits, fleas, spots and divers skin complaints and all other ailments a human body faces.'

Goddammit! A jar of that should keep a man alive forever! He looked for the price. Two dollars a jar! Monstrous!

He turned away, laughing to himself, and then his nerves tensed. Coming towards him were the two men he would rather not face. Jed Crawford and old Pete! And they were talking heatedly.

Trust old Pete to speak his mind, whether it be boss or trail hand. Pete's mouth would get him into trouble someday.

Jed Crawford was listening intently and neither man looked his way. As they came nearer, Saul heard Jed say, 'I don't care a damn what you say, Pete, you're getting too old. You should have taken him up on his offer.'

'But Jed, how long have I worked for you?'

'Goddammit, Pete, that's not the point!'

And then they were face to face and Saul waited for their reaction. If any two men should recognize, they should!

They looked at him and moved out of his way and went on arguing.

Stunned, Saul turned and watched them amble away down the street. Jees! It felt strange, not being rumbled by men he'd lived and worked alongside for days on end. It boosted his confidence.

He was grinning when he walked into the gunsmith's and looked over the collection of guns. He could afford the latest Colt and chose an Army Colt .44 calibre. It handled snugly and felt good in his hand and, when he fastened on a new holster, there was no drag as it came smoothly out of the leather. He bought a box of shells and packed the lot into his valise.

Then, looking around at the collection of

knives, daggers and machetes, he saw the collection of swordsticks and knew that a swordstick would be the finishing touch to his new look.

There were many from which to choose, plain hickory, polished hardwood or ebony with a silver knob and a band of wrought silver just below the shaft. It was well balanced; a lethal weapon for a gentleman to carry. He bought it.

He was now ready to home in on Charlie Breckon and to do so, he must make the acquaintance of Miss Nell Fullalove.

The place known as the Red Garter was a brothel, a very opulent one, catering for the elite of the city and goldminers who'd sloughed off their rough manners and were now pseudo gents expecting the best attention that gold could buy.

The man on the door was a gorilla, but amenable when he saw the size of the tip being waved under his nose.

'I have business with Madame.'

'Yeah, don't everyone?' growled the big ape. 'You can come in and wait. Madame Yvette is with a client right now but go in the first door on the right and the girls will take care of you.'

'Thank you.'

The cocktail of odours hit him when he opened the drawing-room door. It was a large room, noisy with chat from clients and girls getting to know each other, and the heat generated by them brought out the strong perfume, body odours, garlic and the combined smells of rich food and liquor all mixed with smoke from cheroots and cigars. Above all, there was the musky scent of sex.

The room was done in red and gold. It was rich and opulent with overstuffed chairs and S-shaped love seats and everywhere there were small tables with posies of flowers and decanters of wine and long-stemmed wineglasses. Very elegant.

There was a row of young ladies of all colours, all beautiful and wearing eye-catching gowns that appealed to a man's eye, scooped low, the girls' bosoms threatening to pop out.

They were smiling as they looked at him, assessing him, watching for any reaction. They were like a litter of kittens, ready to scratch each other in order to get their claws into him.

He waited. A comely young girl in a dark dress and frilly white apron brought him whiskey on a tray. He smiled and thanked her. It was good whiskey, not the usual rotgut. This was a classy establishment, run on gold.

Then, an enormously fat woman was standing before him. Her rolls of fat were confined in a tight purple satin bodice and basque which made her look grotesque. The gown fell away in a mass of material around huge hips and accentuated her girth. She wore feathers in her hair and was smoking a strong cigar.

When she smiled, her eyes disappeared into the puffy fat that was her face. She tried to look coquettish and a cluster of blonde curls pinned behind one ear bobbed and bounced over a fat shoulder.

Saul had a moment's terror. Surely she didn't expect. . . ? Her words relieved his panic. She wasn't a practising whore. She was the madame.

'Good evening. Ben tells me you are looking for amusement and companionship and you need my help. May I see your credentials and know your name? We are very particular about new members to the Red Garter. I must protect my girls. It is only right and proper. You understand?'

'Of course. I have a receipt from my bank. Will that do? And my name is Rhymer, Saul Rhymer, and I'm looking for dinner with an amusing companion and possibly entertainment afterwards.'

'Good.' For a long moment she scrutinized him, then nodded and her wide smile was back. She leaned over him, narrowly smothering him with her huge bosom, and whispered in his ear. 'Is there anyone you fancy sitting on the banquette? They are all available. All are well mannered, good conversationalists and very talented in other ways.' Her pouting red lips puckered into a suggestive leer.

He pretended to look the girls over and said consideringly, 'It would have to be a private room. You can arrange that?'

'Of course. Now, do you see someone special?'

'I was recommended by a friend to ask for Nell . . . Nell Fullalove. Is she available?'

Madame Yvette stepped back and looked at him consideringly. The smiles were gone. She looked doubtful and suspicious.

'Ah, now we have a problem. She is waiting for a client.'

'I would pay well.'

Madame's eyes gleamed. 'How much?'

'Three times the going rate.'

'Make it four and she's yours!'

'Done!'

Now she was smiling again and showing yellow, crooked teeth.

'Dear boy, a man after my own heart who can make a quick decision and has the wherewithal to back it up!'

'Thank you. You are very kind.'

'A maid will take you to the room and there will be a bottle of champagne on the house while you await her. You may also choose your menu for dinner. We have a famous French chef who left France under a cloud – something to do with poisoned snails, I think – but he's a good cook. You will experience a gourmet's dream.' She turned to leave him and then paused. 'You can pay in gold?'

'Yes, Madame. No problem.'

'Good. Then you must have recently returned from the goldfields?' He inclined his head. 'Ah, I thought so. A good spender. We shall make this a night you will never forget!'

SEVEN

Saul was halfway down the bottle of champagne when the door of the small room opened and Nell Fullalove stood framed in the doorway. She made a pretty picture in rosy gauze silk edged with lace, pink feathers in her brown hair.

Saul was at ease, the champagne doing its work. He raised his glass in a toast.

'Ah, at last, little Nell! Come in and share the rest of this champagne with me.' He belched. 'Excuse me, m'dear, haven't had champagne in a long while.' He grinned at her. Slowly she came towards him.

'You asked for me especially. Are you a friend of Charlie Breckon?' She appeared perturbed. 'Charlie isn't going to like this when he finds out I've been with you.'

Saul waved his free hand airily. 'Who will tell him? I shan't.'

She looked around uneasily. 'There are spies all

around us. He owns half of this place and we all must please him. Even Madame is in awe of him.'

'Come, you needn't be frightened. I'll look after you.'

She raised her eyes to his. 'I'm not frightened for myself. I'm frightened for you. He's very unforgiving and he has a lot of power.'

Saul poured her a glass of champagne and refilled his own.

'Relax. I can deal with him.'

She laughed, looking interested. 'You're either a very brave man, or you're just foolish.' She took a sip of wine then said softly, 'But I like the look of you. I don't want you to get hurt.'

'Come and sit by me and we can get cosy.' He patted the place on the couch beside him. She slid down and he put an arm about her shoulders.

'There now, that's better, isn't it? I can feel you relaxing.'

She looked mischievous. 'It's the wine. It always goes to my head. Another glass and I'll . . .' she hesitated, then said softly, 'well, maybe not. I must remember he will come after the card session is over. You *do* know I am committed to him later?'

'Yes, Madame made it quite clear.'

'And you don't mind? Why not choose one of the other girls and keep out of trouble?'

'Because I wanted to talk to you, that's why.'

'Oh, just talk? I thought. . . .' She bit her lip.

'I'm sorry. I knew about you and Breckon and I want to know all about him.'

'And what makes you think I'll talk about him?'

'This.' Saul held up a fat roll of bills for her to see. Her eyes widened.

'It must be important for it to be worth that much! Why are you interested in him?'

'That's my business!'

She scowled at his tone but fortunately there was a knock on the door and a waiter pushed a loaded trolley into the room. There was the rich smell of cooked squabs and lobsters in a nose-twitching sauce with a selection of vegetables and a tureen of mixed fruits with a figure of a swan done in ice-cream sitting on top. There were two more bottles of champagne in an ice bucket, and on a small silver stove stood a china pot of steaming coffee.

'Madame wished me to tell you that everything you ordered is there and that if you need further attention, you should ring the bell over the fireplace. I also wish you a good night!' He hovered until Saul fished out a bill for his trouble.

'It smells good. Shall we eat?'

They ate and they talked, and Nell overcame her reluctance, especially when she thought of the fat roll of bills. She could even leave Nebraska City and make her way downriver to

Independence or Jefferson City, depending how generous this very attractive man was. As for Charlie Breckon, he could go to hell. She was sick of him anyway, with his cruel streak and meanness about money. She was more curious than ever to find out the connection between the two men.

'Have you known Charlie very long?'

He stared at her as he cracked a lobster claw.

'Can't leave it alone, can you? The less you know the better, my girl.'

'You're a gambler, aren't you? I can smell a gambler a mile off. He's cheated on you. That's it, isn't it?'

Saul smiled. 'Actually, it's the other way round. I cheated on him.'

She stared. 'I don't believe you! I never heard of anyone stitching him up before! You're either a good liar or a good poker player!'

Saul laughed and reached for the second bottle of champagne. The cork popped and the fizz shot into the air. She caught the flow deftly in her glass.

'I might as well make the most of this. Us girls usually get the house wine.' She giggled and belched, the well-bred tones fast disappearing as she downed the wine and held out her glass for more. 'To hell with the bastard! He doesn't have a pecker worth damn all! Jees! What a girl has to do to get him going! Sometimes it takes all night and if he's lost a few dollars then wham! it's uphill all the way!'

Saul looked at his pocket watch. It was well after midnight.

'When is he likely to come tonight?'

She laughed drunkenly.

Saul shook her until her head snapped up and her blue eyes rolled upwards.

'Nell, listen to me. When will he come?'

'Oh, soon . . . very soon.' She snuffled and sank forward, her face hitting her bowl of fruit and ice-cream.

'Jesus!' Saul exclaimed and lifted her head up by her hair. Her face was a mask of chopped fruit and dripping ice-cream. She looked gross.

Swiftly, he lifted her in his arms and, pulling aside a hanging curtain, saw that it hid a bed, already turned down for the night. He laid her down gently and covered her.

It was best that she was unconscious. It would make the confrontation easier.

Then he moved the table from the doorway and positioned his chair, prepared to wait.

He yawned and stretched and looked at the gold watch dangling on its chain. He must have dozed. He got up and looked behind the curtain. The supine figure was lying with mouth open, every now and again giving a little grunt, her bosom heaving as she did so. Poor Nell. She was obviously not used to champagne.

He returned to his chair and waited.

Then, when he'd decided he'd estimated Breckon's reactions wrongly, the door burst open and he was standing there, the big doorman behind him. His face was red, a business-like Colt in his hand. He looked around the room and saw the closed curtain.

'Watch him!' he said in an aside to the doorman, who stood grinning in the doorway. Breckon marched over to the curtain and slammed it back so hard the brass rings rattled together.

He looked down at the sleeping Nell who still had traces of pudding on her face where the napkin Saul had used had missed its mark.

'What's going on here, and who are you?'

Saul drained the last of the flat champagne into his glass, raised it elegantly to toast Breckon and drank.

'To you, Mr Breckon, for having good taste in women!'

Breckon stared at him. 'How do you know my name?'

'Nell told me who her . . . er . . . protector was, before the champagne hit her. She's a very amusing companion for a lonely man who would have preferred poker, but, alas, who doesn't know the right place to look for a high-flying game!'

Breckon scowled and lowered the Colt.

'You mean you and she . . . didn't. . . ?'

'My dear sir, we'd not finished dinner when she succumbed. A gentleman doesn't take his trousers off before a good meal and Madame's chef is not to be taken lightly.'

'Hmm. I've never come across a situation like this before. Why did you ask for Nell's company?'

Saul shrugged. 'A passing acquaintance mentioned what an amusing lady she was. I was lonely. A good companion improves even the best meal, don't you think?' He looked towards the curtain. 'I'm afraid my evening is over. I might as well pay my dues and go back to my hotel. I leave early in the morning.'

He lifted his valise from the side of his chair and opened it in full view of Breckon making sure he caught sight of the gold-edged certificate lying on top of the leather pouches and the stack of greenbacks. He counted out several gold pieces and left them on the table.

'There, that will be enough to settle my bill.' He snapped the valise shut and stood up. 'I'll bid you good evening.'

'Wait! Just a moment. Is it too late for you to play poker? I can introduce you to the most exclusive card room in Nebraska City, if you so wish.'

Saul's eyes brightened.

'My good sir, it's never too late. A high-flying

game can go on all night and if Lady Luck is playing fair, then it may go on all the next day. Have
you the stamina for that?'

Breckon stretched tall, a ripple as of a grated
nerve passed through him. There was something
about this well-turned-out elegant bastard he
didn't like, and then there was the voice . . . it
reminded him of something or someone, but he
couldn't place it.

'Oh, I've got the stamina, if you've got the gold.
In this room I have in mind, we only play for gold.'

Saul laughed and opened his valise again.

'Gold? I'll show you.' He opened his pouches and
from one he poured gold dust into his hand before
returning it meticulously so as to not spill a grain.
He rattled his pouch of gold pieces and finally
tipped his bag of raw gold nuggets on to the table.
'That do for you?'

Breckon stared at the nuggets gleaming a dull
yellow in the dim light. It was a sight that always
excited him. It brought on the gold-fever that was
always just below the surface. The sight almost
gave him sexual excitement. It was nearly as good
as climaxing with a woman – and a damned sight
more private. He looked up at Saul who was
watching him narrowly.

'Where did you get these?' He put out a hand
and picked up the largest piece that weighed in at
more than a pound. He turned and twisted it,

looked at it beside the flickering lamp and gasped at its purity.

Saul laughed.

'Do you think I'm going to tell you? You underestimate me, Mr Breckon.'

'Who are you? You never gave me your name.'

'Does it matter? I've got the gold, let us play poker.'

'The house assayer must assess each nugget. We start with twenty thousand dollars' worth. Is that all right by you?'

'Twenty thousand dollars is fine by me, but my nuggets have already been assayed. I have a list and the pieces are numbered.' He smiled. 'You must appreciate that an impartial assayer is the best man for the job. Not that I don't trust your assayer, but mine was done officially at the Nebraska Corporate Bank.'

He took out of the valise an official list on headed paper and at the same time knocked the certificate to the floor. It fell at Breckon's feet. He stooped and retrieved it and laid it on the table. There was no way he couldn't recognize it for what it was.

'You own your own gold-mine, Mr . . . er . . . ?'

'Yep! I've left a good team working it. I'll be back in the spring with supplies and their cut in dollars. It's a good claim; we'll all end up millionaires before the seam runs out.'

Breckon licked his lips. 'I think we'd better go play poker!'

Saul smiled as he followed him out of the door. Find a man's weakness and play on it. That was the only bit of advice his father had given him that was any good. He'd never forgotten it and, by God, he'd found Charlie Breckon's weakness!

He rode in Breckon's buggy and they stopped in front of an imposing white adobe residence built in the Spanish style. It was a little way out of town and stood in its own grounds which stretched down to a narrow stream.

The short drive was pebbled and at the front neat lawns, very green, betrayed the fact they were watered frequently. The place breathed luxury and wealth.

Inside, the square hall was a vista of blue carpet, gold-framed mirrors, potted palms and gold velvet banquettes with small tables and cuspidors. Above was a huge crystal chandelier with a hundred candles flickering in the draught from the open door.

They were met by an imposing major-domo, who, at a flick of his fingers, summoned up a page who took their hats and Charlie Breckon's cane. Saul refused to give up his swordstick, making the excuse that he needed its support for a sprained ankle.

Then they were being ushered into the Gold

Room, the holy of holies, and the men sitting around the tables paused in their play and inspected the newcomers.

'Charlie! You're back! Wasn't the lady willing tonight, or was there someone else?' A man who reminded Saul of a buccaneer, stood up and laughed. 'Introduce your friend. We could do with some new blood!' He pointed to two vacant chairs at his table.

Saul looked around as he took his seat opposite the man. He counted eight tables, all in use. There was a long bar at which several men stood drinking and in one corner was a discreet alcove where a man sat behind a mahogany desk.

Breckon said softly as he saw Saul's glance, 'He's the assayer. He'll be over to take your gold when we get settled.' Then he looked at his friend. 'Meet Joe Walsh, ship owner and entrepreneur. Has a finger in many pies. A good man to know.' The man smiled and leaned over the table to shake hands.

'And your name, sir?'

Saul saw Breckon watching him closely.

'Rhymewold, Mathew Rhymewold at your service.'

The man nodded. 'May I introduce my partner, Hans van Domme.'

Saul nodded to the blond, thickset man beside him.

Then when they were seated, a waiter came from the bar with four glasses and a bottle of whiskey and after their first drink the assayer, who was a little fat, bald-headed man with white, pudgy hands came and stood respectfully beside him. Saul looked up.

'Good evening, sir,' said the assayer, in a soft, discreet sort of way. 'May I see what you are offering for collateral tonight, sir?'

'Of course.' Saul opened his valise and produced his raw gold nuggets and placed them carefully in a row. Then he brought out his two leather pouches of gold eagles and the dust.

The eyes of the other three men were fixed as if seeing a vision of El Dorado. Breckon licked his lips and the man Walsh turned brick-red. Van Domme caught his breath.

Saul smiled around at them, pleased at their reactions.

The assayer put out a hand to pick up the largest nugget the size of a rock. Saul caught his wrist.

'Not so fast, mister. I know exactly what this lot is worth. I've got the assayer's findings from the Nebraska Corporate Bank, so I'll give you twenty thousand worth in return for your tokens. The rest stays with me.'

The man looked at Charlie Breckon. It was plain to see that the assayer was Charlie's man.

Saul wondered how many gold-mining gamblers had been cheated of their gold when the night turned into a drinking orgy and caution was forgotten.

'Have another drink.' Charlie was smiling and pouring more whiskey into Saul's glass. 'No need to worry, Amos. I've looked over the official list signed by John Bender of the Nebraska Corporate Bank. We can trust Mr Rhymewold, I'm sure.'

The assayer bowed. 'I'll get the chips.'

He came back with a tray of chips and a brass-bound redwood box that had a large key fitted in the lock. On the lid was a number seven in brass.

'May I count out your chips, sir?' He proceeded to do so, leaving them in piles on the wooden tray. Then, pushing back his cuffs in a deliberate fashion to show there was no monkey business, he took the nuggets Saul had selected and checked them on the manifest list and deposited them in the box.

The rest of the gold plus the large rock which had fascinated the onlookers was now safely back in the valise. Saul put it carefully at his feet. He was ready to play.

Charlie Breckon held the bank. He opened a new deck of cards, shuffled them expertly and dealt. The game was on.

The chips were a hundred dollars a throw. The game started cautiously as each man took the measure of the other. Fortune went all ways. Saul was careful. He was watching the state of play and analysing each man's speciality. His brain was working overtime, memorizing numbers, watching, considering and noting give-way signals and facial tics.

For an hour they played and they were evenly matched, not winning much nor losing. Lady Luck was being benign to them all.

Then it was as if a signal was triggered.

'Another bottle over here, waiter,' Charlie Breckon called, and as they waited for it, van Domme and Joe Walsh both left the table and went to the privy. Charlie joked.

'Can't hold their piss. Like a couple of women, they are.'

'Liquor takes some men that way. How about you? You want to go too? You needn't worry. I'll not touch the cards. I don't need to.'

'What do you mean by that?'

Saul shrugged. 'As I said, I don't need to doctor the cards. If you count them, you'll find two short.'

'Good God! You mean, they . . . ?' Charlie Breckon was flustered.

Saul nodded. 'Go on, count them before those two come back.'

'But . . . but . . . .' He licked his lips.

Saul looked grim. 'If you don't, I might think you already knew! So count them!'

The Chiseller

Charlie reluctantly took the pack and counted. Saul was right: two aces were missing.

'Call for another deck!'

Saul waited to see what Breckon would do when the other men returned. It was interesting to watch.

'All right, you fellers, we know what you were up to and as we've been friends a long time, I'm going to forget this incident if you shake those aces down, right now!'

The startled men looked at each other and then at Breckon.

'What the hell . . . ?' said Joe Walsh.

'I know you did it to test out Mr Rhymewold's ability, but he was on to you both. We've got no mean player here, boys.'

So, he was passing it off as a test, was he? Saul thought grimly. Well, they were going to pay for it!

'I'm playing one last hand, gentlemen, and I'm playing it good. It's my turn to call.'

'Let's pour the drinks first.' Breckon poured four generous measures and lifted his in a toast. 'Here's to the best man and may he live long to enjoy his winnings!'

He drank deeply. Saul barely touched his; he needed a clear head.

'I doubt if you'll be able to match my stake,' he said tauntingly, and drew out of his vest pocket the forged deed of a gold-mine which stated he

The Chiseller

had the right to mine plot number nine consisting
of one acre of ground at Goldstream Bluff in the
State of Montana. He put it into the centre of the
table. The men stared at it. Joe Walsh picked it up
and examined it closely, noting the gilt edge and
the copperplate writing and the signature in a
sprawly heavy hand.

'My God! I never thought I'd see the day when
a man would wager his gold-mine! You must be
very sure of yourself, mister.'

Saul smiled and shrugged.

'You come up with fifty thousand dollars each. I
reckon the mine's done me good and there'd be no
more hassle going up and down that damn river
to take up supplies. I'm for the bright lights and
the ladies. Yessir! I'm missing both so much it
hurts my guts!'

Breckon lit a cigar while he thought deeply.

'Is there another reason why you're doing this?'

'Nope! I'm just a gambler at heart. It would
please me to journey on to St Louis with my gold-
mine, my gold *and* one hundred and fifty thousand dollars in gold extra, is all!'

Breckon nodded.

'How about you fellers? Do you want to play?'

A long look passed between Breckon and the
other men. Saul sensed their unease and smiled
to himself.

'I reckon I'm in,' said Joe Walsh, but he didn't

sound happy. Van Domme nodded and took another drink. 'It'll clean me out but I can put down fifty thousand.'

Breckon turned to Saul. 'We're in.'

'Right. But before we start I want to see your gold. That was the stipulation, wasn't it? Gold to cover the chips?'

Breckon cursed.

'Goddammit! We'd all have to send to our banks and they're closed. Don't you trust us?'

'As much as you trust me.' He considered. 'You can borrow gold from here. Get your tame assayer to round up one hundred and fifty thousand dollars' worth and we're on.'

Breckon chewed on his cigar.

'What the hell; it'll be all the same in the long run. Hey, Amos, go rustle up a hundred and fifty thousand dollars' worth of gold and charge it up to me, Joe and van Domme. We want to play poker!'

Breckon poured more whiskey as they waited for Amos who stalked disapprovingly down the room and placed three redwood boxes in front of Charlie Breckon.

'There you are, sir, fifty thousand in each box. Should I open up, sir?'

'No need for that, Amos, Mr Rhymewold will take your word for it. Now get us the chips and let's play.'

'No need for that, gentlemen. Just put the boxes

in the middle of the table. It's one hand, remember?'

Suddenly the atmosphere crackled with tension. The room was nearly empty for most of the gamblers were gone. The clock on the wall chimed four o'clock. Saul looked around at them all.

'Time to test your nerve, gentlemen. Let the bidding begin.'

Saul dealt the cards, slowly and carefully. His fingers, graceful and supple played the old game he'd played many times. He knew just where every card was being placed, what it was and what it was worth. There were three tantalizingly good hands dished out and he watched the small tell-tale reactions on the three faces. He knew without looking what he had for himself. He waited for van Domme to start the bidding.

The play was slow and cautious. Sweat dripped from their foreheads. Saul dearly would have liked to go stand outside and breathe in fresh clean air. He also wanted the privy but he would bust his bladder rather than leave the others to confer.

At last came the moment he was looking for. The chips in front of them were used up. They'd doubled their value and stood at $200 a chip.

'Gentlemen, I think it is time to call.'

Joe Walsh and van Domme looked to Breckon

for guidance. A signal Saul failed to see decided them.

'I'm out, ' Walsh said, and threw in his cards.

'I pass. Far too rich for me,' muttered van Domme, dropping his cards in front of him.

'So it's you and me,' grinned Breckon. 'I'll throw in my last chip to see you!'

Saul fanned out his cards.

'A royal flush in hearts,' he said quietly.

Breckon's triumphant face changed as he threw in his own hand, so near but not good enough.

'God damn you to hell!' he roared. 'How the devil. . . .' He stopped as Saul's Colt appeared just above the table top.

'Now we won't do anything hasty will we, Breckon?'

They stared at each other until Breckon's eyes dropped.

'I think it's time to check the gold. Your Amos can find me a bag to pack it in.' He glanced at Amos who was standing stock still looking uneasy. Saul frowned. 'Maybe we should open up first and take a look.' He pointed the gun at Amos who picked up the keys to the boxes and slowly came to the table. The man was shaking. 'Open up, feller!'

Joe Walsh and van Domme watched impatiently. They wanted the whole sorry episode over. Breckon watched uneasily with a hard glance at Amos.

The man unlocked all three boxes and stood irresolute.

'Well, open the lids, man!' Saul ordered coldly. 'Let's just see what kind of assayer you are!'

The lids came back. The men stared at the contents and suddenly all hell broke loose. Saul's Colt barked and Amos fell to the floor. Joe Walsh and van Domme dived to the floor and Breckon leapt upright and scrambled for his gun as his chair went over with a crash.

'God rot you, Rhymewold,' he yelled, and as Saul twisted to face him, Breckon's gun exploded harmlessly into the ceiling.

'You cheating bastard, Charlie Breckon,' Saul shouted, and tossed off a shot which missed as Breckon bolted to the door. Then Saul was covering the other two men.

'Get up. You two are going to rustle up one hundred and fifty thousand dollars to make up for these stones that that worthless shit stuffed into those boxes and you're doing it now, so, move!'

The other cardplayers watched. It was none of their business, but the word would go round that Charlie Breckon had welshed on a gambler and put up a parcel of stones for gold collateral. His status in Nebraska City would now be lower than a snake's.

Joe Walsh pulled a groaning Amos to his feet.

'Give me the key of the vault. You stupid fool! Why didn't you use the gold reserve?'

Amos cast him a venomous look.

'You're the stupid fool! There is no gold reserve!'

For a moment, Joe Walsh stood stunned and then, without warning, clipped Amos on the jaw.

'You bastard! You let me believe. . . .' Then he whirled towards Saul. 'Come along, I'll get you what you want and to hell with Charlie Breckon! I hope it breaks the sneaking slimeball! I'll break his head when I catch up with him, and as for this lump of dogshit, I'll deal with him later.' He gave Amos a vicious kick in the ribs.

He called a waiter to bring a carpetbag and Saul, still suspicious of some trick, followed him, his Colt trained on Joe Walsh's back.

But Joe Walsh was seething and if Charlie Breckon had been around, would have killed him on the spot.

'Here, take it and get out,' he grated to Saul when he'd opened the vault and counted out the packets of new bills. He laughed bitterly. 'I've been pards with Charlie for ten years and never dreamed he would rook me. Now I might as well clear out whatever's left and get on the first steamer to St Louis!'

Saul took the heavy carpetbag and, carrying his own valise, reckoned he needed a cab.

'Get that waiter of yours to order Breckon's cab

to the entrance. I'm going to need help with this lot.'

'Yeah, you need help all right. If I know Charlie, he'll be waiting to ambush you, and not because of what you're carrying but because you humiliated him in front of the town gamblers. He's a bad loser is Charlie.'

The cab pulled up at the entrance and Saul, looking both ways for a possible hold-up, dived for the door and threw in his bags and jumped in.

'Where to, mister?' an old voice croaked.

Saul gave him the name of the hotel where he and Amy Grainger and the children were staying.

'Right, mister. I can go the long way round and keep to the main streets or I can cut through the alleys; unlit but takes half the time. Which is it to be?'

'You get me there safe and quick and there'll be a bonus for you, so it's up to you!'

'Then it's the alleys for sure.' The old man cracked his whip and the horses got under way.

Saul sank back into the leather cushions and sighed with relief. Once at the hotel he knew he would be safe. He glanced down at the two bags. There was a fortune at his feet. He would deposit it into the bank tomorrow along with the gold and have it all transferred to his bank in St Louis.

He grinned when he thought of Charlie Breckon and the way he had fooled him. He only wished he'd disclosed his identity and had a proper showdown with the murdering bastard.

He was aroused from his reverie by a distant shouting way behind him. They were moving along a narrow lane filled with refuse with only a flickering lamp here and there to pierce the murky blackness. He put his head out of the cab.

'Where are we, driver, and what's going on back there?'

'We're crossing town, mister. Those hooligans back there are from the waterfront. We're running parallel with the levee. Drunk as skunks they are. We'll soon be out of reach of the varmints. In any case I always carry m'old shotgun just in case.'

'Maybe you should have stuck to the main streets, old-timer.'

'I'll get you there safe and sound, never fear!'

But the old man was wrong. The slug came out of the darkness and slammed into the old man's arm. The horses reared and bolted flinging the old man into the dirt.

Then suddenly there were men with staves, shouting and yelling, and two stalwart rivermen tried to grab the frightened horses.

Saul cursed as the men beat on the sides of the cab.

'We know you're in there, Charlie Breckon,' a stentorian voice shouted. 'You're not getting away from us! We want our pay and we want it now!'

The cab came to a standstill and Saul put his head out of the window and stared at the bunch of men before him. Some carried burning torches and the flickering light lit up swarthy, sweaty faces, bearded and fierce and deadly determined.

'I don't know why you want Charlie Breckon, but I'm not him. I want him too!'

'It's Charlie's cab. He's inside. You can't bluff us, mister!' someone at the back shouted.

A man built like an ox tried to open the door.

'We'll soon find out what's going on,' he growled, and then stood back as Saul's Colt rapped him on the knuckles.

'One more move, mister, and I'll blast you to hell!'

The man leapt back, nursing his knuckles.

'If Charlie's in there throw him out!'

'He's not and I'll plug the first man who says he is!'

EIGHT

The big man glared suspiciously at Saul. He raised a hand and the tumult died down as the men behind him watched and listened to the heated conversation.

'You willin' for me to take a look?'

'Yes, but no tricks. This gun has a hair trigger.'

'Right. You open the door and I'll take a gander. No mess!'

Saul opened the cab door and sat back, Colt trained on the opening for fear of a sudden assault. The big man looked around and took his time, then scratched his head.

'You be in the right of it. How come you have his cab?'

'I commandeered it. The bastard's out there somewhere. I needed to get to my hotel and you're stopping me.'

'You mean he might come after you?'

'Yep, and if we meet face to face, there'll only be one of us left to tell the tale.'

149

'Like that, is it? Then maybe we're both on the same side. I'm Cap'n Ben Greenham and some of the boys out there are my crew. I own the *Riverbelle* and that welsher Charlie Breckon's ducked out of paying me for freightage up to Fort Benton and back. He owes us ten thousand dollars and, by God, if he hasn't got it, we're gonna take it out of his hide!'

'I'm sorry I can't help you.'

'But you can! I'll drive you to your hotel and my boys will follow. If the bastard is out to get you, he'll come looking for you there and we'll be waiting. If he see his cab, he'll come like a bird back to his nest! And when we get him. . . .' He stopped and gave a low laugh and Saul's spine prickled. He was glad he hadn't Captain Ben Greenham for an enemy.

'If that's what you want, Captain, I'll go along with it. I'll be the bait!'

'Just let me get rid of these hangers-on and I'll have a pow-wow with my boys and then we'll make for your hotel.'

He turned and raised the wicked-looking belaying pin and hollered in a stentorian voice, 'Come along, boys, let's get rid of this riff-raff. We don't need these bilge rats.' He turned on the ragged bunch of dock labourers who had followed the crew for excitement, booze and the chance of a free-for-all. They scattered like the wind as the crewmen laid about them. They went off cursing and nursing sore heads leaving the crew grinning at Saul.

'Right, boys. Follow the cab. I'm driving this gentleman to his hotel and with the devil's own luck, we might run into Mister Charlie Breckon, the welshing gutter rat!'

Saul sat tight, Colt in hand. He didn't quite trust the captain and he'd trust him less if he got an inkling of what Saul carried in the two bags. At the moment he could be passed over as a business man with a valise and all his worldly goods in an innocent carpetbag. He wanted to keep it that way.

They drew up outside the hotel and Saul sighed with relief. He'd feel better when he finally checked into his room.

Captain Ben grinned when Saul stepped down, pulling the bags with him.

'You got a mighty lot of weight in those there bags, mister! Just what might be your business with Charlie Breckon?'

'That's not your business, Captain. Let's just say we don't see eye to eye on certain matters and I humiliated him in public.'

Captain Greenham scowled.

'Maybe I made it my business bringing you here. I reckon you be a gambler. Am I right?'

'Among other things.' Saul hefted the Colt significantly. 'And I don't stick at poker!'

The captain eyed the valise.

'I also reckon you be holding some of Charlie Breckon's gold in that there case. Now, how about doing the decent thing and giving us the ten thousand Charlie owes us? It would be a token of friendship, like.'

'Now why should I do that?'

'Because there's more of us and one man's chances against six are not odds that any gambler should take!'

Saul laughed to hide his inner shaking. God damn the man! So near to the safety of the hotel and now this. He could sense the growing hostility.

'You're right. One against six is long odds, but I'll take someone with me. Who'll be that man?'

'He will!' a stentorian voice roared from the shadows, and then came the flash of a weapon and the report. Suddenly Captain Greenham stiffened and arched his back. His eyes widened in surprise as he was punched into the air to fall with a heavy thud. Blood welled from the wound. He twitched and lay still.

Saul watched with fascination, momentarily paralysed at the suddenness of it. The captain's men scattered as footsteps sounded in the darkened street.

Then Charlie Breckon walked into the flickering light coming from the hotel foyer.

'So we meet again, Mr Rhymewold, if that is your name which I very much doubt.' A business-like Peacemaker was trained on Saul's middle. 'Do you mind dropping your gun? I like to be in charge of things. You understand me?' Saul dropped his gun at his feet. He could feel the small weapon nestled in a shoulder holster, so near and comforting.

'Perfectly.'

'I am puzzled by you, Mr Rhymewold. I am sure we have met before, but where is beyond me. Have we met before?'

'The paddle-steamer, *Star of the West*. You were on board. Remember? The ship you helped to wreck?'

Breckon's eyes narrowed.

'Ah, you were the young gambler who befriended the Grainger family.'

'Mrs Grainger died because of you and your associates.'

'Too bad. Fortunes of war, you might say,' Breckon answered coolly. 'I didn't recognize you. That was remiss of me.' He eyed the valise and the carpetbag dumped at Saul's feet. 'Joe told me before he died that you'd taken your winnings in greenbacks from my vault. You know you finished me in this town? I want what is mine, you interfering, cocky bastard! I also want that deed to your gold-mine. Where is it?'

Saul moved a hand towards his vest.

'May I?' Without waiting for an answer, he drew out the crisp parchment sheet and waved it into the air. 'This what you want?'

Breckon drew a sharp breath. 'It might just save your life.'

Saul shook his head. 'You're lying, Breckon. Nobody humiliates Charlie Breckon. You're a bad loser and I know how your mind works.' Suddenly he tore the paper in half, again and again until it was in small pieces and flung them into the air.

'What the hell do you think you're doing?' Breckon sprang forward in a fury.

'It was just a piece of paper, Breckon. A counterfeit. Not worth the ink and gold leaf on it!'

'Why you. . . .' Breckon's Peacemaker exploded as Saul dropped to the ground and rolled away. Breckon aimed again, but Saul was sheltering behind the cab, the wheels beginning to turn as the frightened horses started a headlong gallop.

Then Saul was exposed and Breckon stood over him, laughing and savouring the moment before shooting him.

'If you want to say a prayer, Rhymewold, or whatever your name is, say it quick.'

There was the sound of an opening sash window from above the hotel foyer. Charlie Breckon heard it, but it did not register as he stood over Saul.

Saul licked his lips. If only he could get at his small derringer. . . .

Then from above came a chamber pot, plus its contents, which hit Charlie Breckon on the head. He swayed, stunned, wiping his wet face. Amy looked out of the window. Saul grinned with relief.

'What the hell. . . ?' Breckon spluttered.

'You've been shit on for the last time, Charlie Breckon!' Saul took careful aim with the little derringer and a small neat hole appeared between Breckon's eyes.

Saul looked down at him and turned him over on to his back with his foot.

'That was on behalf of all those who died out there on the river. May you rot in hell!'

Later, when the bodies of Greenham and Breckon were carted away, and the local undertaker well paid to dispose of them, Amy clung to him.

'I'm sorry if I made a spectacle of myself. I hope you'll forgive me. You see, when I looked out of the window and saw you being held up by that most dreadful man it was the only thing I could think of . . . .' She stopped and blushed. 'It's a terrible thing to talk about.'

'Then don't, but I assure you, it was the best thing to do.'

'But not what a lady should do!'

'I'm glad then you're not a lady. I'm glad you're

you.' He held her close and kissed the top of her head.

'So you're not ashamed of me?'

'On the contrary; I'm proud of you.'

'Oh, Saul, I *do* love you!'

'What about us getting married before we leave for St Louis? I'm thinking we should take the overland trail. I don't think I could face another steamer passage. What do you think?'

She nodded, her head pressed into his chest. Her voice was muffled. 'Anything you say, dearest. Our home will be wherever you take us.'

'You'll have no regrets?'

'None. My life is in your hands.'

He smiled. Life was good.